FINAL SEASON

ALSO BY TIM GREEN

FOOTBALL GENIUS NOVELS
Football Genius
Football Hero
Football Champ
The Big Time
Deep Zone
Perfect Season
Left Out

BASEBALL GREAT NOVELS
Baseball Great
Rivals
Best of the Best
Home Run

AND DON'T MISS
Pinch Hit
Force Out
Unstoppable
New Kid
First Team
Kid Owner
Touchdown Kid
The Big Game

FINAL SEASON

TIM GREEN

HARPER

An Imprint of HarperCollinsPublishers

To the four brothers, forever!

Library of Congress Control Number: 2021936193
ISBN 978-0-06-248595-3

Typography by Kate Engbring
21 22 23 24 25 PC/LSCH 10 9 8 7 6 5 4 3

First Edition

Sleepovers made Ben throw up.

"There's nothing to be nervous about." With an effortless flick of his arm, Ben's older brother Rich zipped a football at him. It spun so fast the laces whistled. "You need to expand your horizons."

The ball stung Ben's hands, and he winced on the inside as he caught it.

"What horizons did *you* have at twelve?" he said with a salty edge in his voice.

"You're dropping your elbow; you gotta keep it up." Rich flashed his smile and took a few easy steps toward Ben, holding his arm up and pointing to his elbow before he launched himself into a full sprint.

Ben turned and took off. He made it halfway across the lawn before Rich tackled him from behind.

"Do you have horizons? Huh? Yeah?" Rich pinned him to the grass and dug a thumb into Ben's armpit.

"Okay . . . Okay . . . Stopstopstop! Okay, okay, okay!" Ben thrashed and howled with laughter.

"Okay, what?" Rich wiggled his thumb deeper.

"Okay, I have horizons! I have horizons!"

Rich rolled off of him and lay back in the grass. Ben caught his breath. Giant puffy clouds littered the blue summer sky. It was a perfect day. School had ended just last week, and the months of July and August lay in front of him like two giant chocolate cakes, each slice a treasure unto itself.

"I told you, I'll come get you if you need me to. You text me, and I'll be there. I promise." Rich tore a handful of grass from the lawn and tossed it so it landed on Ben's face. "This way you don't have to get nervous and you don't . . . you know, have an issue."

Ben sputtered and spit and grabbed as much grass as he could before returning the favor. "*You're* an issue."

Rich made a grab at him, but Ben slipped out of reach and quickly got behind a clump of sharp-needled juniper bushes that he kept between them by dodging this way and that.

"Okay, I'm being serious now." Rich silently surrendered, picked up the football, backed up, and zipped it to Ben. "Do this thing. Tell your friends before you even go that I may need you to cover for me with Dad so that I can stay out late with his G-Wagon. You know that he won't mind me using it if it's to pick you up. That way, if you do want to bail, no one knows but you and me."

"No questions asked?" Ben narrowed his eyes and fired a perfect spiral.

"No questions." Rich rubbed some dirt off the ball on the front of his UCF football T-shirt. "You just text me 'bailing' and I'll pull up in five minutes."

"Five?" Ben scowled.

Rich threw the ball back. "It's a three-minute drive to town. Jessica and I will be right here watching a movie. Keep your elbow up higher this time."

"Why do you care if I sleep over or not?" Ben made sure his elbow was up as he released the ball.

"Hey, that's it!" Rich caught the pass, grinning. "Circle of truth? Dad babies you too much."

Their dad was a former NFL defensive lineman, and now an attorney and author who had written a couple books. He was quick to smile, and he smiled a lot, but he could also become a raging thunderstorm in the blink of an eye. He never got that way with Ben, though. His four older siblings seemed to delight in pointing out how he was "babied" because he never saw the wrath of their father directed at him.

Ben's insult was all Rich needed to hear. He turned and began to walk away. What he hadn't told Rich was that Ryan Woodley would be there, and when Ryan was at a sleepover, trouble was never far behind. If he said that now, it would look like an excuse.

"Hey, get back here! We just got your elbow right!"

Ben didn't slow down.

"See? Just what I said! If I ever walked away from Dad, he would have lifted me up off my feet by the collar and carried me back!" Rich had a temper too, and he was letting it show.

"Well, you're not Dad!" Ben picked up his pace because he knew that he was in danger of having a football zinged at him.

Rich had been an all-state quarterback with a full scholarship to the University of Central Florida. A handful of injuries had prevented his college football career from ever taking off, and now he was home and going to law school.

The ball stayed in Rich's hand, and Ben made it inside the house unscathed. He fell onto the couch and took out his phone.

Rich wasn't far behind. "Don't even tell me you're calling Mom. You gotta toughen up."

"I'm texting Tuna, okay?" Ben held up his phone so his brother could see. Tuna was Anthony Tonelli, built like a barrel with feet; kids had taken to calling him Two-Ton Tony. But Tony's personality was as big as the rest of him, and he began calling himself Tuna, which everyone thought was hilarious. "To tell him I'm coming over tonight."

What Ben still didn't say was that he was pretty sure that with Ryan Woodley there, the night would end in trouble.

His stomach got queasy just thinking about it.

Rich pulled up to Tuna's, and Ben quickly got out of the car. Tuna had a big white house on a big green hill. In the front, thirty-foot white columns upheld a flat triangular pediment, reminding Ben of the Greek temple he'd seen in a history book. The house was originally built for President Teddy Roosevelt's sister.

Tuna's dad was a retired investment banker and could afford the giant house that looked down on the lake. Ben made his way around back, where he found Tuna in the boathouse hauling a sunfish out of the water. Tuna removed the hook from its mouth and slipped it into a ten-gallon plastic bucket. Ben peeked in. The surface quivered as dozens of fins fanned the water.

Suspended above two boat slips like a mismatched pair of shoes was a shiny classic wooden boat beside a sleek new speedboat that looked right out of a Batman movie.

"Hey, Ben. Grab a pole." Tuna nodded toward a rack of poles on the wall as he tore a worm in half and pierced its wriggling belly with a needle-sharp hook.

"Nah." Ben looked away from the spurt of blood and guts. "More fun for you."

Tuna chuckled and let the worm plunk into the water before jiggling his pole. He glared at the water. "See that whopper down there? Smallmouth bass. Can't get him to bite."

Ben felt a little thrill at seeing the dark shadow suspended only a few inches off the bottom.

Tuna asked, "Do you think we should put these sunnies in Woody's sleeping bag?"

"Why?" Ben could envision a night of never-ending paybacks.

Tuna glanced up at Ben with a slightly annoyed look on the thick features of his face. "The slime alone would be worth the price of admission, but you tack on the smell and it's an epic prank of the ages. We get it on video, post it online. Don't tell me you don't see it?"

"No, I get it. I get it." Ben peered into the bucket wondering which lucky fish would get to suffocate to death after flopping around with a half-naked Ryan Woodley. Water gently lapped the boathouse piers, and the hint of gasoline danced in and out of Ben's nose. "But the drama. You know. It'll never end."

"Hmm. You got a point." The end of Tuna's pole suddenly whipped down, and the expert fisherman gave it a yank. "It's the Whopper! I got him! I got him!"

Ben saw a silver flash the size of a fireman's boot before

it disappeared under the floor. Tuna gripped the pole like a samurai sword and gave a heroic slash.

The line snapped. The pole went limp.

Tuna's face dropped. "That sneaky sneaker."

Deeply disappointed, Tuna was determined to sacrifice one of the Whopper's friends to his entertainment for the evening. He slowly poured out the contents of the bucket, returning all but the last fish to the water so they could live to fight another day.

Ben's stomach rumbled. "Wanna eat something?"

Tuna nodded. "Yeah, all this fishing is making me hungry. Plus the guys are due any minute."

Up at the house, Tuna left the bucket in the bushes outside the game room, which was how they would go in and out of the house to and from the tent set up under a big shade tree in Tuna's side yard. Upstairs, a dozen pizzas arrived at the same time as Finn Heick and Malik Merit. While the four friends fist-bumped each other, Tuna's older sister, Moira, appeared and removed half the pizzas for her and her friends, who had taken over the deck off the kitchen.

"Hey!" Tuna cried. "Those pizzas belong to us!"

"I'm in charge until Mom and Dad get back." Moira gave him a superior look. "Besides, even you couldn't eat two pizzas by yourself, Anthony."

"Big Tuna can eat two pizzas for a snack between meals." Tuna proudly patted his belly. "Most real men aren't scrawny little weasels like your boyfriend, Mopey Moira."

Moira ignored her brother but slammed the door on her way out.

"Whaddaya say, whaddaya know!" Ryan Woodley shouted, appearing out of thin air with his trademark greeting. Everyone called him Woody. He came up to Ben's chest. He was as light as he was short, limited on the football field to cornerback and wide receiver. Some people said Woody tried to make up for his small size with his big, oversized personality.

The five teammates took their pizzas along with some sodas and installed themselves in the game room, where each of them had an Xbox with his own flat-screen TV. As they played, Ben couldn't help but think that he could have been in the comfort of his own home, with his own Xbox, but without any worries about the trouble that loomed ahead. Their game of choice was *Call of Duty*, and they ran it for hours, until they were stuffed to the gills with pizza and darkness ruled the world outside.

After a final victory, they powered down their machines.

Woody made a big show of stretching his body and loudly groaning. "Whaddaya say, whaddaya know, guys! Who's ready for a real-life mission? Who, huh? Malik? Big Tuna? You guys are always up for anything, right?"

Malik had dark skin and a powerful build. His parents were both doctors and he was the class brainiac, but he had an older brother who lived on the wild side, so there wasn't much he hadn't seen.

"I'm in," said Malik.

"You don't even know what it is," said Finn, giving voice to Ben's exact thoughts. Finn got razzed among his friends for being so skinny and the quietest of them all, but next to Ben, he was the fastest kid on their team and an outstanding wide receiver.

"Tuna is *always* game," said the Tuna, grinning.

"Majority rules," said Woody. "C'mon, let's go. Sleeping bags in the tent, and then I reveal my diabolical—should I say diabolical?—yes, my diabolical master plan."

Ben really wanted to give the whole thing a chance, so he piled into the tent with everyone and rolled out his sleeping bag on the end next to Tuna.

Woody stood in front of the rest, who sat cross-legged on their bags. "Wimple," he said, looking around, grinning. Woody watched *Peaky Blinders* on Netflix with his older brother. The two of them had adopted the same hairstyle as the men on the show, buzzed tight on the sides and long on the top, but slicked back. This meant that later in the day when the gel broke down, Woody's hair hung in his face like a sheepdog.

"Mrs. Wimple?" Malik asked.

"Bingo." Woody made a gun with his finger and shot Malik.

Mrs. Wimple was a well-known grouch who handed out detentions in the middle school lunchroom like toothbrushes at a dental convention. She lived with her adult son on the edge of town in an old, run-down two-story farmhouse surrounded by thick swatches of pine trees. On one side of the lot was an ancient graveyard, and on the other, a farmer's field. Her son was a horror show of tattoos, black clothes, and piercings all over his face. Kids in town gave him the secret nickname of "the Weirdo."

Woody reached into his duffel bag and carefully removed a garbage bag containing three egg cartons. "These, my friends, are no ordinary eggs, but eggs carefully heated and tenderly preserved over time to render each one an insanely potent stink bomb."

"What about the Weirdo?" Finn's voice was hardly a whisper.

"The Weirdo is what makes it fun," Woody explained to Finn like he was a simple child. "The thought of him prowling around in those pine trees or busting out of that house like some crazy zombie is what makes the hair stand up on the back of your neck."

Hearing that, Ben wasted no time fishing his phone out of his pocket and secretly texting his brother Rich to come deliver him from this madness. The five teammates pulled on sweatshirts as the night had cooled off, and they'd also want the protection for pushing through the bristly pine trees. Ben took his time and envisioned Rich driving their father's black Mercedes SUV down West Lake Road.

He fully expected to see his brother pulling into the driveway as they rounded the house. When nothing was there, he stopped in the driveway and said, "Guys, wait up, my sneaker."

Ben bent down and fiddled with his laces, keeping an eye

on the street for the flash of headlights.

Tuna began walking back. "Yo, Ben. You need me to tie your shoes? C'mon, buddy."

"No, I'm good." Ben stood and walked as slow as he dared toward their staring faces.

When Ben caught up, Woody patiently said, "You good now, Ben Attack? You okay?"

Ben looked up the road and saw only empty blackness. "Yeah, I'm good. It's just that thing I was telling Tuna about . . ."

Everyone turned their eyes on Tuna.

"Huh, what?" Tuna wore a big empty stare with a mouth that slowly opened and closed like the fish he was named after.

"Tuna, come on." Ben scolded his friend. "My brother? Me being ready to help cover for him if he's out late with my dad's G-wagon?"

Ben stared at Tuna, pleading with his eyes to go along with the story. He hadn't had a chance to say anything earlier, and he was kicking himself now.

"Oh, for sure! Totally!" Tuna turned to the others. "He did. Ben told me before he even came over that he might need to bail, and I said no problem."

"Well, if he calls you, you gotta go, but he didn't yet, did he?" asked Woody, peering at Ben in the soft light of the stars.

Ben pulled his phone out to look at his text notifications. No response from Rich. "Ah, no." Ben denied the urge to search the street for oncoming lights. He gave himself a mental kick in the butt. He should have said he needed to stay at Tuna's because his brother might come without warning, but it was too late for that now.

"All right," Woody said, "hoods up. We stick to the shadows. Follow me."

They dashed through backyards, pausing behind hedges before crossing streets, and hugging the grass whenever they tripped a motion sensor light on someone's garage or back porch. Finally, they stood in a loose circle breathing excitedly in a dry ditch beneath a rusty mailbox whose sloppy white letters read: WIMPLE. The driveway disappeared instantly into the thick wall of long-needled pines that reached for the stars.

Woody slung the garbage bag off his shoulder and dug in to share the wealth of stink bombs. Using the saw blade on his pocketknife, he deftly cut one of the egg cartons in half and handed one each to Tuna and Ben.

"You guys take the sides." Woody pointed across the driveway. "Tuna takes the north side, and Ben's got the south. You and me will cut through the cemetery. I'll take the back."

Woody rapped his knuckles on Ben's chest, then tucked a carton under his arm and handed the other to Malik. "Malik and Finn got the front. Two of you to make it faster. Now, we want to hit the windows if we can, but don't worry if you miss. Either way, the Wimp and the Weirdo are gonna have a lot of stink on their hands."

Woody checked his phone. "Okay, it's ten twenty-three. Everyone get into position and we'll launch the attack at exactly ten forty-five. Anyone jumps the gun gets a double-fisted high wedgie. We gotta make sure everyone is in place, so text me when you get there, and unless you hear from me, we launch at ten forty-five."

Finn raised his hand. "What about after? Where do we, you know, meet up?"

Woody's smile glowed, reflecting the distant streetlight. He spoke in an excited whisper. "Once you've thrown all your eggs, you fly outta here as fast as you can. We don't meet up till we're back in Tuna's tent. That way, if anyone gets nabbed, it'll be just one guy. The rest will get away clean. Do you love it, or what? I got goose bumps. Look."

Even in the weak light, Ben saw that, indeed, Woody's arm beneath his rolled-up sleeve looked like a Thanksgiving turkey before going into the oven.

"Goose bumps? Who wants goose bumps?" asked Finn.

Woody rolled his eyes. "People pay money for these things, Finnerty. People make fortunes on fright. Ask R. L. Stine, Stephen King, Chucky, all of 'em, millionaires."

"Pretty sure Chuckie's a puppet," said Tuna beneath his breath.

"Finn, you good, or you need me to hold your hand?" Woody didn't hide how annoyed he was.

"Good," Finn mumbled.

"All right, boys." Woody grinned and held out a fist. "Let's bring it in for a break. 'Stink' on three, ready? One, two, three . . ."

"Stink!" they all whispered with the intensity of a hushed locker-room cheer.

"C'mon, Ben. You're with me in the graveyard." Woody scrambled up out of the ditch.

Ben followed without comment, but his mind was racing with how he could get out of the mess. He quickly checked his

14

phone, but still no answer from Rich.

Ben and Woody had just entered the graveyard when the headlights of a vehicle crept over the nearest hill.

"Duck!" Woody sounded gleeful.

They each pressed themselves tight behind an ancient head-stone. The car slowed, and Ben's mouth went dry before the car rolled past them, picking up speed.

Woody popped up. "Thriller."

Time betrayed Ben, as usual, going at light speed when he needed more of it. Before he could think, Woody was wishing him luck and pointing into a wall of branches, dark and forbidding.

"Don't forget. If the Weirdo comes for you, you get outta Dodge. Just drop your eggs and hightail it. We can't win the championship this fall without our star quarterback. Ha. Ha!" Woody gave him a gentle shove and ran off as Ben stumbled into the blackness of the pines.

Ben's nose filled with the smell of Christmas, the deep, rich scent of pine. The long needles swept his cheeks like soft brushes. His fingers were soon sticky with sap as he groped blindly, pushing branches from his way. He wondered why he hadn't seen the house yet. Then, off to the right, a stick snapped.

Fear squeezed Ben's stomach. He uttered a broken cry and bolted.

His heart hammered his chest wall, and his breathing came in short gasps. He swam through the pine branches until his arms and legs were gassed. He stopped and forced his breathing to slow. He had no idea where he was, or which direction he faced. The blackness pressed in on him. He battled back his panic, but in the silence, he thought he heard a noise. He felt just like the time he'd touched the wire fence that contained his older sister's horses, a buzz from his toes to his ears.

Whoever it was, whatever it was, they had stopped moving.

Ben strained his ears until they hurt. His mind raced. He wanted to whisper Woody's name. He could have stumbled into his friend's area. Also, a prank within a prank wasn't beyond Woody. What made Ben afraid he might wet his pants, though, was the thought that the person no more than twenty feet away from him was the tattooed Weirdo with a pipe or a hatchet.

The noise of a car driving down the road gave Ben his bearings in an instant, and he didn't think about what to do next. His legs launched him through the trees, heading for the graveyard and ultimately back to Tuna's. He could hear his pursuer behind him, snapping branches, gaining ground. Ben flailed at the web of needles and bows with his heart ready to burst.

His feet tangled. He fell, and the force of impact lit his brain like a lightning bolt.

His body kept going. He was up and flying in an instant.

Too late.

The hood on his sweatshirt stretched, then held. The bottom of the hood bit into his throat.

Ben was yanked off his feet.

He fell backward, and someone clapped a strong hand over his mouth.

Ben's captor shook with delight.

Laughter leaked from his throat like a punctured inner tube.

"It's me, you goof. What are you clowns up to?"

"Raymond?" Raymond was Ben's other older brother, older than Rich, in fact married with a job. "What are you doing? You choked me, you idiot!"

"Aww! What is that smell?"

"My eggs," said Ben. "You made me break them."

"Just as well. Rich said I was supposed to save you from your friend's shenanigans." Raymond thumped his back. "This way."

Ben tucked in behind his brother's wide muscular back until they broke free from the pine trees.

"Hey, how'd you know where I was?" Ben brushed off his hoodie.

Raymond held up his phone. "Find My Phone app."

"Wait, that's for if I lose my phone."

Raymond laughed. "That's what Mom and Dad want you to think. Don't look so offended. We've all been through it. It's part of the price for having a free phone. They like to know where you are."

"Oh." Ben followed his older brother through the graveyard to his black Ford Expedition parked on the side of the road. He had just opened the door when a bloodcurdling scream split the night. Several more yells of lesser intensity floated up toward the stars before a storm of whacks sent a thrill through Ben's thick frame.

Raymond was already in his seat, and he fired up the engine. "C'mon. I don't want anyone running out of the house and getting my license plate."

Ben jumped in with feelings of relief mixed with guilt and disappointment.

"What's wrong, Bo?" Raymond kept his eyes on the road.

Bo was a nickname that only his family used. He got it when he was little and they were all watching *Lord of the Rings*. Rich was teasing him about being little like a hobbit and called him Bilbo's brother, Benbo. He didn't mind. He liked the idea of being a hobbit, so the whole family took to calling him Benbo, which turned into just Bo as he got older. It reminded him how close they all were, and how they did so many things together as a family.

"Just that all the guys are going to be talking about this until Christmas, and I'm gonna be the guy who chickened out. I should never have listened to him. Expand my horizons, he said."

"Who?"

"Rich. He was supposed to pick me up right away if I texted him." Ben shook his head in disappointment.

"Well, don't feel bad," his brother said. "Jessica's brother's car broke down, and he asked me to cover for him. I didn't know I was supposed to race to the scene, but I pulled you out of the fire in time."

"Yeah, you did. Thanks." They turned onto the main road through town. "Swing by Tuna's, would you? I gotta get my stuff."

"Not that it matters, but what are you going to say to your friends?" Raymond turned onto West Lake Street. Ben didn't bother pointing out Tuna's house; it was so enormous that everyone in town knew where it was.

Ben borrowed a pen and a piece of scrap paper from the console between the seats. They pulled up into the driveway. He hopped out of the truck and left the door open. "I'll be right back!"

Ben dashed around to the side of the house to where the tent was. He quickly gathered his things and scribbled out a note to Tuna. He left the tent and took three steps toward the truck before he stopped. He unslung his big duffel bag from his shoulder and let it drop to the grass.

Ben turned and jogged to the back door where he and Tuna had entered the house earlier that day. He found the bucket in the bushes right where Tuna had left it. The fish thrashed against the bucket soaking Ben's pants.

"Doggone it, fish!" Ben hoisted the bucket and staggered down the lawn and into the boat house. With all the sloshing and the thrashing, Ben was entirely soaked below the belt. He went to the back of the last concrete boat slip and dumped the bucket, setting the fish free and denying his friends some more excitement, and certainly laughter. Still, he felt lighter on his feet as he jogged up the hill, grabbed his bag, and hopped into Raymond's truck. As they drove, Ben took out his phone and texted Tuna, covering his tracks, saying his brother showed up and took him home, which was the truth. He signed off quickly by saying he was shutting his phone down until the morning.

They pulled into the lane where both Raymond and his wife, Cara, lived. Ben and their parents lived a little farther down the road, right on the lake.

"Wanna stay at my place?"

Ben had his own room in Raymond's brand-new home. "Nah, I wanna see Mom and Dad."

"Uh, buddy." Raymond slowed the truck to a stop at the end of his driveway. "Mom and Dad aren't going to be home till tomorrow."

"No, tonight." Ben pointed down the lane.

"They had to stay one more night." Raymond's voice was different. His brother sounded scared. "They had to see a different doctor."

"Oh." Ben knew his dad had gone to New York City with his mom to see a hand specialist. His dad had had three operations over the past few years to try and fix some of the damage he'd done to his body during his eight-year NFL career with the Atlanta Falcons. After nerve relocations in both elbows and a thumb fusion, his hands were still giving him trouble. His dad never made much of the aches and pains from football.

Whenever his knees, neck, back, or whatever old injury bothered him he'd say, "Football paid for this house on the lake, so . . ."

Their house wasn't as large as Tuna's, but it was pretty big and nice. It sat on a bluff, and they could see for fourteen miles to the south end of the lake.

Ben forgot about his friends and rotten eggs and runaway fish.

If the hand surgeon was sending their father to a different doctor, then the problem wasn't his hands, it was something else.

Something that was making Raymond's voice tremble.

Something very bad.

Ben tossed and turned all night. He watched the sun come up through the bedroom window, then walked downstairs to find Raymond eating cereal at the kitchen table.

Raymond looked up from his phone and forced a laugh. "Hey, what's up, Bo? How'd you sleep?"

"Crappy."

"How 'bout some cereal?"

Ben nodded and got himself a bowl and a spoon and sat down. "What kind of other doctor?"

"Here, I'll get you some orange juice." Raymond escaped the table, grabbed a glass, and flung open the refrigerator door, hiding from Ben's view. Ben waited until the juice was in front of him.

"Thanks." He took a drink. "What kind of doctor, Raymond?"

Raymond ran his fingers through his hair. "A neurologist."

Ben felt a frozen sickness pass through his body. "Why? What is it?"

"It's probably not anything." Raymond turned his head away, suddenly interested in the tree outside the window.

"Is it CTE?" Ben knew all about CTE. Chronic traumatic encephalopathy. Concussions and repeated blows to the head oftentimes resulted in CTE, a disease that essentially rotted a person's brain, making them crazy and sometimes even suicidal. A college teammate and friend of their father's had killed himself because of it. After a long NFL career, he had come back and broadcasted the Syracuse University games on the radio and worked for the university, so everyone kind of knew him. In the back of Ben's mind, he secretly feared that happening to his dad. He knew from dinner-table talk that their dad had more than ten concussions in his football career.

"No, I don't think so." Raymond turned his eyes on Ben.

"Then what?" Ben sighed with relief.

"Eat your cereal. Then I'll thrash you in *Madden*." Raymond forced a grin.

"In your dreams." Ben ducked as Raymond threw a soggy Honey Nut Cheerio at his head.

Raymond's wife, Cara, appeared in her robe with sleep in her eyes. Cara was pretty, with dark eyes and long brown hair. She pointed her finger at the floor. "You better be picking that up."

"You do it." Raymond smirked at Ben.

Cara rolled her eyes but didn't seem mad at all as she headed for the Cheerio.

Raymond scrambled and beat her to the soggy circle. He scooped it up and popped it into his mouth.

"You're gross, and lucky." She kissed him, then veered off to the coffee machine.

Ben knew Raymond was sandbagging him, but it was easier to buy into Raymond's carefree attitude than it was to worry about their dad all day when there might be nothing wrong.

The rest of the morning and into the afternoon, Ben had a great time with both his brothers and their girls down by the water. They all went swimming and tubing, then took the boat into town for fried fish sandwiches and milkshakes at Doug's restaurant. But in the back of Ben's mind, he was haunted still by worry. However, when they returned from their lunch in town, Ben saw something waiting for him on the dock that made him forget about the mystery with his dad.

Tuna had run his Sea-Doo right up onto the shale stone beach. He had helped himself to a can of Cherry Coke and was waiting patiently in the sunshine with a pair of pink sunglasses that he must have stolen from his sister. He'd chosen to sit in one of the two lounge chairs that everyone kind of knew were Ben's parents' chairs. Blubber hung over the band of his swimsuit, and he had tied his T-shirt around the top of his head like a pirate.

Guilt washed over Ben for ditching his friends during their rotten-egg adventure last night, but he waved happily to his friend. Tuna only raised his chin in reply. Raymond pulled the boat into its slip and cut the engine. Ben hopped out and approached Tuna from behind. As Tuna's thick legs came into view, Ben noticed the dark water stain discoloring the thick orange cushion beneath Tuna's wet suit.

"Hey, Tuna, wanna get out of the sun a little? You're gonna be a lobster if you sit out here much longer." Ben poked his friend's pink arm, resisting a poke in the belly because that would give Tuna another thing to complain about.

Tuna glanced at his arm before turning his chubby cheeks back toward the sun. "What really happened last night? And don't tell me your brother."

Ben didn't sit down. He still hoped he could get Tuna to move without directly asking him. Ben's parents taught them all that when they had a guest, to treat them like they owned the place.

"You can ask him if you want." Ben pointed at his brother.

"The Tuna wasn't born yesterday." Tuna remained in the same position, staring up at the sun. For all Ben knew, his friend's eyes might be closed.

Ben finally sat down on the edge of the other lounge chair facing Tuna. He remained silent for a while, the gentle sounds of waves and distant motorboats poking fun at the turmoil inside Ben's mind.

Ben cleared his throat. "So how did things end up last night, anyway?"

Tuna lowered his pink sunglasses and looked out over the top of them. "You mean the same guy who abandoned his teammates and then shut off his phone is suddenly concerned?"

"Okay, here we go." Ben gave Tuna a dirty look that didn't seem to bother his friend. "I mean, I told you from the start that I might have to go. Don't tell me you didn't explain that to the guys."

Tuna pushed the glasses back up his nose and sighed heavily.

"I told them what you said. Woody got a little hot. The other guys didn't seem too upset."

"Too upset?" Ben's hands flew into the air.

"Well, we were on a mission, you know." Tuna's lower lip poked out of his face.

"We were egging a house. That's vandalism, not a mission."

"You're a lawyer now too?" Tuna whipped off the pink glasses and heaved his body up and twisted it so that he was sitting face-to-face with Ben. "Do you know that Woody almost got caught? The Weirdo chased him all the way to the firehouse."

"No, Tuna, I don't know anything because I wasn't there, okay? Shoot me."

Tuna put his hands on his knees and leaned forward. "Take it easy, will ya? I'm the one who defended you, even though you let my fish go."

"Who said I let your fish go? It could have been your sister, or one of her friends." Ben nearly choked on his guilt.

A sly smile crept across Tuna's face, and he made a fist, which he thumped on his chest. "C'mon, bro. You're tough on the football field, but you're soft right here and you know I'm right."

"Whatever." Ben pretended to be more upset than he really was because he wanted to level the playing field between him and Tuna. He knew he had a soft heart. Since as far back as he could remember, he was okay being that way because his dad said that they had that in common, and that made Ben as proud as he could be.

"Aww, don't get all sensitive on me." Tuna chucked Ben's shoulder. "I forgot about it anyway until this morning. We were laughing too hard at the Wimp's house smelling like a fart factory."

The two of them shared a smile.

Then Tuna frowned. "Hey, you threw your eggs, right? Cuz I went to bat for you. Woody went on and on about his stinky eggs."

"Woody's a stinky egg." Ben paused to let Tuna have a laugh. "You can tell Woody that every one of his eggs got smashed."

Tuna grinned and thumped Ben's shoulder. "Attaboy."

Ben stood up. "Hey, want to hang out with us?"

Tuna looked over at Ben's brothers, who were hard-nosed football coaches to him. "Nah, I gotta get back. My sister's been nagging me all morning about the tent killing the grass."

Ben walked Tuna to where the dock split off. Ben's brothers both called out to Tuna, and he said hello, addressing them both as coach. Ben waved to his friend as he growled away on the Sea-Doo, and then he joined his brothers and their significant others.

They all lay out in the sun for a few hours until Ben heard his father's deep voice calling to them all from the path leading down from the house. "Hey, what's this? Everyone lounging around?"

Ben's heart galloped, but when he and his brothers looked up, they all froze in their lounge chairs.

Ben raised a hand to shade his face from the sun. His frozen feeling turned to all-out stomach sickness. His fish sandwich bubbled up into his throat in a brew of ice cream and acid. His dad wasn't alone. His mom was walking with him, hand in hand.

Ben's mom and dad kissed and hugged all the time, but

they didn't usually hold hands. The only other time he'd seen them do that was when they told him that they were going to have to put Lucy, his dog, to sleep.

When their father stood among their chairs, all three brothers got up to kiss and hug both parents.

They each exchanged the words they always had whenever they came or left each other. "I love you."

When the brothers had returned to their seats, Ben saw that his dad clasped their mom's hand so tight that his jawbreaker-sized knuckles were white.

"How was the drive?" asked Raymond.

"Great, we took seventeen. No traffic." Their dad forced a smile. "Look, I've got some good news, and some bad news. . . ."

Ben gripped the edges of his lounge chair and hunched over to keep from throwing up.

"As you all know, I've been having a lot of problems with my hands. My doctor referred me to a neurologist. I had a few tests done and, well . . . Bad news is I've got ALS." Ben's dad choked on those last three letters, and his eyes glistened with tears that didn't spill. "Good news is that I am going to have the best ALS doctor in the world. Doc Smart trained under her, and he connected me to Dr. Merit Sucovich. She's working on bringing all these new medicines to do trials with people, and I'll be right there on the front line. I think they've got to find a cure soon. So I'm gonna be around for a long, long time. Right, hon?"

Ben's mom looked up at his dad. She stood no higher than his shoulder. She opened her mouth to speak, but nothing that Ben could understand came out. She nodded her head, though, so at least that was something.

But Ben remembered last week his dad started to slur his

words. And he lost his balance a few weeks before that.

Ben looked at his older brothers to see their reactions because maybe he was wrong. Maybe ALS wasn't something as horrible as he thought.

Raymond's face was white, and his mouth was stretched in horror. Rich wore a strained smile. He was always the upbeat one.

"Can you still coach our team?" The words escaped Ben's mouth before he could stop them. Everyone stopped to stare at him. He didn't know what to say, how to explain that the words just came out.

His dad smiled. "Of course."

Everyone seemed to relax, except Ben's mom. "Are you serious?" She stiffened and looked up at Ben's dad with a scowl. "After what they told you? Are you crazy? Ben isn't playing football anymore."

"What?" Ben sat up straight. He felt his jaw drop.

"Yeah. He is. And we're coaching." Ben's dad waved a hand in the direction of his two older sons. "We made a commitment."

Ben's mom shook her head. "I can't believe you."

"This is kids' football." His dad threw his hands in the air. "I smashed my head thousands of times, against guys who were three hundred pounds and could dunk a basketball. These are *kids*. They can't create the force it takes to do the kind of damage I did."

"Kids get concussions sometimes, John."

"Yeah, and they get concussions sometimes on the playground or on a bike or a skateboard. Come on. Can we leave this alone? I've had enough."

Ben was surprised when his mom went along with the suggestion. She was usually a pit bull.

"Hey," said Ben's dad, "let's take a boat ride to the end of the lake. Want to?"

"I'll go." Raymond got up from his chair. "Come on, Cara."

Ben was surprised Raymond spoke up first. He never wanted to go on the boat.

"We're in." Rich was already up and folding his towel.

They all piled into the boat and were soon cruising at a high speed toward the south end of the lake. Ben sat in the front with Rich and Jessica facing backward, so Ben could see his dad's grin. With one hand on the wheel and the wind in his face, Ben's dad, with his long, dark hair blown back, looked like he was in heaven. It felt like the conversation from a few minutes ago was a bad dream, and nothing was really wrong, and Ben wondered if ALS wasn't as dire a disease as he first thought.

The crystal clear aqua-green lake was calm, and there were relatively few boats out considering the blue sky and the blazing sun. Ben saw a boat go by that was similar to theirs, an open bow cruiser that had the power to pull skiers or multiple tubes, or just to get from one end of the seventeen-mile lake to the other in less than a half hour. His dad was slowing down when the wake of the other boat rocked their own.

Ben's dad's legs collapsed beneath him like matchsticks. "John!" Ben's mom shrieked. "Dad!" Raymond darted forward but was too late to keep their dad from hitting his head on the corner of the windshield and collapsing onto the floor.

Raymond hooked his arms under their dad's armpits and hoisted him off the deck.

"I'm okay! I'm fine!" Ben's dad swatted Raymond away.

"Dad, you're bleeding." Raymond grabbed a towel and handed it to him.

"Oh my God." Their mom covered her mouth with a hand.

Blood gushed from a cut in his scalp and ran down the side of their dad's face and neck, soaking his gray polo shirt. He dabbed at it with the towel. "This is nothing. No big deal. I'll sit for a few minutes—it'll stop. Then we swim. Look at that water."

They waited a few minutes, and Ben's dad kept pressure on his head. It turned out that it was only a small cut, and it stopped bleeding quickly.

"Okay, let's go." Ben's dad was a big man, and he stayed in shape by lifting weights, walking, and eating right. So when he headed for the swim platform at the back of the boat, no one was going to stop him. He stumbled but used his momentum to flop into the water.

Their dad bubbled to the surface spraying water like a whale. "The water's great! Come in!"

Except for their mom, who was still rattled by the fall, they all jumped in. Ben opened his eyes underwater and could see everyone clearly, with the aqua-green water reaching into the depths. Their dad dropped the anchor off the back of the boat. Ben watched it disappear into the gloom, the rope stretched taut. They were in more than three hundred feet of water, so the anchor hung like a man on the gallows.

Their dad grabbed a mask and snorkel from one of the many compartments in the sides of the boat and announced that he'd be the judge of who did the deepest dive. He had a container with different colored hair clips that they would clip on the anchor line, and he handed them out. Their dad then slipped back into the water, and the contest began.

Ben tried, but they all knew that Rich was the likely winner. Raymond would come close, and sometimes even pull off a victory. The two of them were best friends but complete opposites and always fierce competitors. If it was a strength contest, Raymond usually won. If the contest involved speed, Rich usually won. Ben just enjoyed the show, knowing that no matter how hot things got, they'd all be friends ten minutes later.

Rich did win, and they all dried off in the sun and wind on the boat ride home. From behind his sunglasses, Ben secretly watched his dad for signs of ALS, but to his relief, there were none. He stood with one hand on the wheel. In his other hand was one of those unusual-sounding German beers he loved. He wore a smile on his tan face, without a care in the world.

When they docked at home, Ben noticed his older brothers hovering around their dad as he stepped off the boat. The girls, including their mom, announced their plan to lie out in the sun.

When they had all safely unloaded, Rich said, "Let's go work on some pass plays."

"You guyths go. I'm anna juth sit wid yer ma." Their dad turned quickly and headed for the end of the dock, where he and their mom usually sat in their padded lounge chairs. He only stumbled once, and it might have been nothing. But his slurred words were back, and Ben wondered if they were here to stay.

The three brothers headed up the steps toward the house.

"Bo," said Rich, "should we work on the deep routes, or the bootleg series?"

"How about a little of both?" said Ben.

"You're the man . . ." Rich replied.

Ben swelled with pride. There were times when his brothers treated him like one of them, presuming he too would be a football star. Raymond held the single-season sack record at their high school, and Rich was an all-state quarterback with several records of his own. Both brothers helped their dad coach Ben's team—Raymond was the defensive coordinator and Rich coordinated the offense.

"Hey, how many beers did Dad have?" Rich looked right over Ben at their older brother.

Raymond frowned and shook his head for Rich to stop talking. "One."

Rich continued despite his older brother's dark look. "One? Sounded like a lot more than that."

"Can that make Dad slur his speech? That's been happening a lot lately," Ben said, glancing at his oldest brother just in time to catch the end of a throat-slash gesture telling Rich to stop talking for real.

His brothers stayed silent, and Ben didn't press. But even as they worked on the plays that would hopefully lead to an undefeated season, he wondered what Raymond was trying to hide from him. He wasn't at his best during their practice session, but he wasn't at his worst either. Rich kept nagging him to put more spin on the ball, but his accuracy was pretty good.

When they ended their session, the two older brothers headed back down to the water.

Rich gently shoved Ben from behind. "Come with us, Noodle Arm."

"I'd rather have a noodle arm than a noodle brain." Ben shoved his brother back, hard, but Rich barely stumbled.

"Oh, the shade!" squawked Raymond.

"You mean the shade I threw on him?" Rich took a bow.

Raymond stared at Rich for a moment. "Uh, no."

Ben laughed and peeled away, dodging the football Rich threw at him.

Ben didn't run, but he didn't walk either. He was eager to get to his computer. He took the stairs two at a time up to his room, closed the door behind him, and sat down at his desk.

Immediately, he turned his computer on.

He was going to google ALS.

Ben's fingers trembled as he typed those three simple letters, ALS. Up popped a slew of websites. The first page was full of ad sites. He had to go to the second page before he got to some real sites, mostly medical schools at universities. His lips quivered as he clicked on the first one and began to read.

It was like a horror movie—he was afraid to look but he had to.

First of all, his dad's falling and his slurred speech were two of the ALS symptoms mentioned in every website he looked at. Second, his dad would eventually be paralyzed and die from the disease. Third, there was no cure.

Ben kept reading, and the horror continued.

The life expectancy for someone with ALS, or amyotrophic lateral sclerosis, was three to five years, but in some cases the disease progressed faster. Ben did the math and choked. Even if his dad wasn't exaggerating about a cure to make them all feel better, which is just what his dad would do, Ben probably wouldn't be out of high school before . . .

He'd had enough reading. Ben's eyes scanned his bedroom walls and came to rest on a framed photo of him, his dad, and brothers with Arthur Blank, the owner of the Atlanta Falcons football team, and their star receiver, Julio Jones, down on the field before a game. Ben wondered if they'd ever make it to another Falcons game.

The computer screen stared back at him, and he returned to the main Google page.

At the very bottom was a site that caught his attention: ALS Action.

His heart skipped a beat. Action meant there were things to be done. He grabbed the mouse and clicked on the site. His eyes scanned the screen. But there was only more of the same. Frustrated and upset, he growled at the screen, ready to throw the mouse into the wall.

Then, there at the bottom, it read: "Important Recommendations for ALS Patients."

His heart pounded as he read. There was a drug called riluzole that helped slow the progression of the disease. This excited him, so he devoured the rest of that section. When he came to the last few sentences, he had to stop and read them over.

The final recommendation was that anyone who had ALS should immediately get his or her affairs in order. When he read that more carefully the second time, his stomach turned over.

Ben knew that meant to make a will, and plan for your funeral.

For the next few weeks, no one in Ben's family talked about his dad's condition. And even though he noticed his father's speech getting worse, Ben was able to bury his worries beneath the summer fun of riding WaveRunners, fishing, and training with his brothers. On the weekends, there was an unwritten rule that everyone would gather at his parents' place, unless they had something else going on. That meant not only Ben's brothers, but his two older sisters were at the dinner his mom cooked for them one Sunday evening after a day in the sun.

Brea, Ben's oldest sister, was a veterinarian—Dr. Redd she liked to remind everyone—and Ben didn't blame her. She'd spent three long years on a Caribbean island with her fiancé, Mike, and then a final year at Wisconsin to get her degree and train for her job. His other sister, Rosie, went to Harvard, and his brothers complained that their father was way too lenient on her.

Ben liked when everyone was there and the big round table just off the kitchen and overlooking the lake was full. Everyone had their seat at the table and they rarely switched, so Ben sat between Raymond and his mom. Her seat was empty until she brought one final dish from the kitchen, an enormous bowl of steaming spaghetti with meatballs and sausages. Along with some grilled broccoli and Parmesan cheese, and a fresh tomato and mozzarella salad, it was his dad's favorite.

"All righ, who's unna say du blessin?" Ben's dad gave a hard look around the table. Finally, his eyes came to rest on Ben.

Ben looked around. Raymond kicked him gently under the table. He was the youngest, and that seemed to mean that not only did he have to go to church with his dad on Sundays, he was expected to say grace if no one else volunteered.

Ben sighed. "Dear God, thank you for this food, thank you for our family, and thank you for our . . . our . . . our good health. Amen."

"Amen," said the rest of his family in unison.

Ben noticed his sister Brea giving him a dirty look. Rich had the same frowning face. Those two were always uptight. Raymond and Rosie, like their father, were already chewing their spaghetti. His mom was taking a sip from her wineglass while she studied his dad.

Ben picked up his fork and dug in. Ben loved his mom's spaghetti.

They were halfway through their meal when the talk turned to football.

"I've got a new defense for Penn Yan," Raymond said.

Penn Yan were their archrivals. It was another small town on one of the Finger Lakes in Upstate New York. Unlike Ben's team, they were bruisers, big, strong, and mean. The biggest player on Skaneateles was Tuna, and he was hardly mean. Ben was the next biggest, and he was the quarterback, so it didn't really matter how mean he was. Penn Yan was the only team they hadn't been able to beat for the past four years.

Rich playfully choked on his can of cranberry seltzer. "I gotta hear this."

Raymond picked up his can of lemon seltzer and toasted Rich. "We all know offense sells tickets, but defense wins games."

"Maybe when they wore leather helmets defense won games, but today it's all offense, right, Dad? You know." Rich was getting excited, the way he did when he and Raymond went at it.

Their dad looked up, still chewing. Everyone was watching him. He swallowed, then took a drink of his wine. "Rishard, my boy, I'm sorry da say id, bud defense was, is, an always will be duh secred do winning."

Rich turned red. "You guys played D. That's the only reason. You know I'm right."

"Dell us da plan Raymond. Dell us how we finally gonna bead dem guys." Ben's dad raised his glass to his oldest son.

Ben noticed his dad's speech was getting bad. He didn't understand why it was happening more often now. But his brothers and sisters didn't say anything and kept talking as if nothing was wrong.

Raymond nodded with excitement. "Dad, remember when

you played the Houston Oilers, and Coach Glanville had the corners play man coverage and nine guys up on the line?"

His dad grinned. "Yeah, I—"

"Okay. Okay, just stop." Ben's mom threw her napkin down on her untouched plate. "Enough football. Enough!"

Everyone stared. You could cut the silence with a knife. But his mom wasn't finished.

"Benjamin is not playing football anymore. He's done."

"Whah are you dalking abouw?" Ben's dad looked at his mom like she was from Mars.

"Do I really need to spell it out for you?" Ben's mom had a wild look in her eyes that he rarely saw, and her voice rose to match the look. "How could you even *think* of letting him play? It's dangerous. Look at you. Look at your teammates. Read the paper. Chris Gedney kills himself. Every day it's someone new. ALS, CTE, dementia, Alzheimer's."

"It's totally different." Ben's dad was excited now too, and Ben noticed that he suddenly was barely slurring his words. "When I played, we hit three dimes a day in camp. Every single play I would smash my head into some three-hundred-pound rhinoceros to sdop his charge. I did that, whad? Ten thousand times? A hundred thousand? Ben, he's a quarderback. They barely get hit anymore, and ad this level? C'mon. How can you even be serious?"

"I am serious. Completely." Ben's mom scanned the rest of the table, looking for support. She skipped right over Ben.

"Id's not the same," Ben's dad said. "The game is differen now with all these concussion protocols. Id's much safer."

"I hate to say it, Dad, but it's still not safe."

Everyone turned their eyes toward Rich. Ben glanced at their dad, who looked like a volcano ready to erupt.

"Whad are you even talking about?" Their dad twisted his lips like he'd tasted a lemon.

"I read it. There was this study. You don't have to have a concussion. Just hitting your head is enough. They found that ninety-nine percent of NFL players will have CTE. For college it's ninety-one percent." Rich turned to his older brother. "Bad news for you and me, and even high school players have a twenty-one percent chance. No, I'm with Mom. When Jessica and I have kids, no way am I letting them play."

Raymond wiped spaghetti sauce from the corners of his mouth. His face was bright red. "Where did all this come from? If you don't want to coach with us, just say that. Don't go tearing down the tent 'cause you don't want to dance."

Rich wore an impish grin. "First of all, I'm a dancing machine. Second of all, I am gonna coach, just like you, Brother, if Bo plays. All I'm sayin' is after what I read, my kids aren't playing football. If Bo plays, that's up to Mom and Dad."

Ben had been slowly eating his spaghetti. He swallowed what was left in his mouth and put down his fork. He reached for his can of lemon seltzer, brought it to his lips, but put it down untasted. Rich, the all-state quarterback, the one who spent countless hours teaching him to throw while sharing all the tips he'd learned at UCF from the Hall of Fame coach

George O'Leary, was suddenly against football? Ben sat with his jaw ajar.

Ben's mom turned to his dad. "See? Rich knows. Did you hear what he said? Almost a fourth of high school players. A fourth! And he's not going to let his kids play because he's smart. Who would let their kids play?"

Ben watched his dad's face grow dark. With a motion that was too quick to see, Ben's dad smashed his fist on the table. Silverware danced and sang. Bowls and plates shivered.

Ben's father wore a terrible face as he yelled, "If you or anyone thinks, because I'm depleted by this, this condition, thad I'm gonna be rolled over like some chump, you are wrong. I am committed to coaching this team, along with Rich and Raymond, and Ben is playing quarterback if he wants to. Do you want to, Ben?"

Everyone stared at Ben.

He couldn't speak, but he slowly nodded his head.

"Then that's it. I'm coaching and Ben's playing. Are you guys coaching?"

"I was always coaching," said Raymond.

"I'm in. I never said I wasn't," Rich said.

Ben's dad glared at his mom. "Then thad's it."

Ben's mom returned the glare, and the standoff seemed to last hours. But after a few minutes, his mom, who was tough as a tiger despite being thin and pretty, said, "He can play this season, but this is it."

"He'll play the next year too, if he wants," Dad pressed.

"No, he won't."

"We'll see about that." Ben's dad pushed back his chair, stood up, and walked away, ending dinner.

Football wasn't the only sport Ben played. In the winter, he wrestled, and in the spring, he played lacrosse. Ben's sister Rosie played lacrosse at Harvard, and their parents made a big deal out of that. Ben thought the whole Harvard thing sounded fun, but he liked lacrosse anyway. He played defense, where being big and quick were important. Part of being a top recruit like his sister meant playing on an elite club team in the summer. Lacrosse was a thing for Ben, even before his mom and dad argued about football.

Ben had just finished playing a tournament game for Orange Crush, one of the top travel teams in the country. That was why he was sitting in the back of his dad's G-Wagon while his parents talked about whether they would eat dinner with the team or set out on their own before heading back to the hotel. Ben waited for an opening where he could make a plea for going with the crowd. His friends would be there, Charlie,

Luke, and Reed, the coach's sons, and Tuna, the team's goalie.

Then his dad said, "I juss doan wan people looking ah me and asking quessions, hon."

"No one is going to ask anything." Ben's mom ran the backs of her fingers across his dad's cheek.

He threw a glance at her. "When I've god soda leakin from da corner of my mouth an dribblin down da side of my face? They migh not ask, bu dey'll be talkin'."

"Well, Ben can catch up with his friends at the pool." She patted his dad's leg. "Let's see where we can eat."

"The hotel has a pool? Awesome." In his excitement Ben forgot that it wasn't polite to listen in on other people's conversations. Normally, Ben's dad would have pointed that out with a stern, scary face. It wasn't the first time since he announced a few weeks ago that he was sick that Ben's dad had been a softer, gentler version of himself.

"You wan a shake, Bo?" Ben's dad flicked his eyes in the rearview mirror, and Ben tried hard not to look concerned—he didn't think he meant a shake—maybe steak? "I saw a sign for a LongHorn Shake coming up on the nex exid."

"Oh, I love LongHorn Steak." Ben's mom spun around in her seat so she faced him. "That was one of our favorite places to eat in Atlanta. Your father always got the New York strip steak, and they never let us pay, even though your dad tried to every time."

"Sure," Ben said. They headed off the exit ramp and into the restaurant. Their steaks were not eaten without incident. Ben's dad had a glass of wine with his mom, and after a generous swallow, his dad had a coughing fit, hawked up a wad of

48

steak, and tipped his chair over on his way to the bathroom.

Ben was stunned, but his mom just frowned while she picked up the chair and sat down as if nothing happened. Ben could see some of the other customers staring at them. "Just don't say anything when he comes back."

"Mom, what happened? What's going on?"

Her eyes now glistened with unspilled tears. "The muscles in his mouth and throat are . . . getting weaker. It's why his speech is off, and some of those same muscles help you chew and swallow."

"Oh." Ben didn't know what to say. He wanted to ask how things were getting worse so quickly, but he didn't want his mom to spill those tears.

She reached across the table and grasped his hand. "I don't want you to play football this year, but your father is set on coaching, and I don't want to take that away from him—from either of you."

Ben nodded like he understood, even though he didn't. He picked up his fork, stabbed the meat, and began to saw with the big steak knife they give everyone. Blood seeped from the cut, and it disturbed him for a reason he did not know.

When they got back to the hotel after dinner, the indoor pool was a madhouse. Many of the parents were at the bar. Ben's mom sat, dressed in her jeans and casual blue top, in a lounge chair talking with Luke and Charlie and Reed Lockwood's mom. Ben jumped into the middle of the deep end with a whoop. He came up only to have Charlie dunk him. Gasping, Ben fought to the surface and returned the favor. Luke and Reed were in the shallow end, and they decided to splash him from both sides. After he cried, "Okay, okay okay okay!" the four of them decided to attack their teammates in the hot tub. Afterward, they all had a cannonball contest, which Tuna ran away with.

It was ten thirty when Coach Lockwood came in. "Okay, boys. Everyone out! We got a big game day tomorrow." Like the rest of the team, Ben hopped right out. No one wanted to see what would happen if they didn't obey the coach. Ben's dad was already in the room lying on one of the beds, reading his book. Ben had the other bed all to himself, and he fell right to sleep.

The next morning, they only had time for a quick breakfast before they headed over to the tournament. Ben had a stack of pancakes, something he'd never dream of eating before a football game. Football games, like sleepovers, made Ben throw up. Lacrosse games were intense, but they always felt more like a pickup game in gym class.

The fields were at a small college outside Philadelphia. Old gray stone buildings looked down on the fields from their grassy hilltop. The sun was a hazy yellow, and although it was not even nine a.m., it was already oven-hot. Orange Crush had a tent set up with a tub-sized cooler full of Powerades. Ben dumped a folding chair beneath the tent and hustled out onto the broiling turf for warm-ups.

Their first two opponents were what Tuna called tomato cans. The Orange Crush knocked them over with ease. Games like that were kind of boring for Ben because the Lockwood brothers, who were offensive superstars like their dad, rarely allowed the other team to get the ball. When they did get it, Ben usually checked it out of their sticks if they came to his side of the field. If they got by the defense, Tuna usually saved the other teams' shots. As Coach said, Tuna not only took up a sizable portion of the goal, but he had lightning-quick reactions.

The real competition came later in the day when they faced two elite teams, one from Long Island and another from Denver.

Ben's team beat each of them by a single goal, the Denver team in overtime. By the end of all that, Ben was soaked to the bone with sweat, and dog-tired from running in the brutal heat all day.

The team had pizza at the Hut that evening. Ben went with the Lockwoods because his parents were meeting up with one of his dad's law clients. After pizza, the team hit the pool for a while until Coach blew his whistle at ten and ordered everyone to bed. When Ben got to the room, he heard his dad's snoring before he closed the door. He tiptoed in to find his mom reading under the glow of the lamp between the beds. Ben recalled the days when his dad was the last one to bed and up with the birds. He guessed it was one more thing about his dad's condition. That was his dad's word, "condition." Ben liked that word. It sounded so much better than "disease."

"How was your dinner, Mom?" Ben whispered.

His mom laid her book down on her lap. Her legs lay under the covers and her free hand strayed to Ben's dad's hair. "It was good. The people were nice."

Ben's dad's snoring faded to a distant train whistle. Ben studied him to make sure he wasn't awake.

"I thought he didn't want to eat with people."

His mom looked at the mountain under the blanket beside her. She twirled a lock of dark hair around her finger. "I think it's just people around home. He doesn't want people feeling sorry for him."

Ben nodded. "Coach said if we didn't go straight to bed, we were dumber than a box of rocks."

"Well, brush your teeth, then." She smiled, turned her book over, and began to read.

Ben cleaned up fast and was in bed well before eleven. He wanted to be ready for tomorrow's championship game. There would be plenty of college lacrosse scouts there, and while Ben planned on being a big-time college quarterback on his way to the NFL, it excited him to be looked at by college coaches. But the excitement didn't do him any favors, and he tossed and turned with nerves. And then he began to think about his dad.

After a time Ben realized his hands were clenched. So were his teeth.

He sat up and looked at the shapes of his parents beneath the covers. The sound of his dad's heavy breathing filled the silence. It wasn't fair.

Why?

Why did this have to happen? Ben lay back down, spilling tears on his sheets. He took a deep breath and closed his eyes. He really had to get to sleep.

The alarm shattered Ben's slumber. He bolted up, blinking and pawing at his mom's phone to silence it. The sudden quiet called him back into the warm covers. The AC was blasting. He fell back to sleep in an instant.

"Benjamin." His mom shook his shoulder. "Get up, honey. Let's go."

Ben tried to pull the covers back over his head, but his mom blocked that move like a ninja. With her other hand she began poking his ribs.

"Ahhhh." He rolled over to protect himself. He was awake now, but the chains of exhaustion hung heavy around his neck.

He was a zombie during breakfast.

"You be'er pick id up, Bo." That was his dad's contribution.

He dozed on the ride to the field. When they arrived, his mom looked at him. "Are you okay, Ben?" She mashed her cheek against his forehead. "No fever." She looked at his dad, and he shrugged.

"I'm just really tired," Ben mumbled, grabbing his gear bag. He was dressed for action. Only his gloves and helmet remained in the bag, which he slung over his shoulder. He dragged his stick, a defenseman's long pole.

"Do'n drag your shick," his dad said.

Ben sighed and rested the stick on his shoulder, wondering how he was ever going to make it through. The parking lot was awash in players and parents, as many coming as going, different age groups from all across the country, some playing for championships, some for a third-place medal.

Ben found his team under their tent, hiding from the morning sun, which promised to melt plastic by noon. No one looked half as tired as Ben felt. When Coach Lockwood caught Ben's eye, he frowned. "Hey, Ben," he called, and crooked his finger, signaling for Ben to follow him as he turned toward a field where a game was in full swing.

Coach rested his forearms on Ben's shoulder pads and looked him in the eyes. "Now, these guys are good, maybe the best we've ever seen."

Ben swallowed. His throat and mouth felt stuffed with cotton, so he nodded instead of trying to speak.

"Okay, and they have a middie who's bigger than you and maybe better than Charlie."

Ben's breakfast crawled up the bottom quarter of his throat. He'd never seen anyone better than Charlie. Charlie was quick as lightning and tough as shoe leather. He made magic with his stick, and the ball never betrayed him. Ben looked around for some sign of the team from Maryland who they were about to face. He knew their jerseys were red.

"Ben, I'm talking to you. Are you okay? Did you not listen when I said bedtime by eleven o'clock?" Coach's face wrinkled and reddened.

"I was in bed before eleven, Coach. I just . . . I had trouble getting to sleep."

Coach's anger melted into a smile. "That's how I was. Never slept before a big game. You'll be all right."

Ben wondered how in the world he'd be all right. He felt like falling on his face, but he nodded because whining to the coach would never do.

"Okay, so this kid's name is Heckler," Coach continued. "He's number twenty-seven, and I am gonna have you guard him man-to-man all day."

Breakfast now tickled the back of Ben's throat.

"Why are you looking at me like that?" Coach Lockwood's eyes had that crazy light in them, and he brought his face so close to Ben's that their noses almost touched. "You okay?"

"No, I'm good, Coach. Number twenty-seven." Ben swallowed back his pancakes, leaving a burning trail of acid in his throat.

Coach backed off a bit. "You know I already saw coaches from Notre Dame and Yale. I'm sure they and a lot of others will be watching."

Ben cleared his throat. "Great."

"Right, a big-time opportunity. Glad you're up for it. Let's win this thing." Coach walked away, calling his son Charlie's name.

Back under the tent, Tuna was hydrating himself with Powerades. Two empty bottles lay at his feet, and he had half an orange left in his hand. "Ben!" Tuna called him over with a wave of his head.

When Ben got close, Tuna looked up and spoke in a low voice. "You hear about this Heckler kid?"

Ben looked around. Everyone was making last-minute equipment adjustments. "Yeah. Coach just told me I'm playing man on him the whole game."

"Man? By yourself?" Tuna's mouth fell open.

"That's what he just said."

Tuna looked around before sharing his wisdom. "So I was talking to the Denver goalie. They played Maryland in the Sunshine Tournament two weeks ago in Dallas, and he said they double-teamed Heckler and he still had five goals. Now Coach wants you to handle him alone? I don't know."

Ben waited for Tuna to stop shaking his head. "What's that supposed to mean, 'you don't know'?"

"Five goals bein' double-teamed, and we're only gonna put one guy on him? Do the math. That's ten goals he could score on me, and Teddy DeMore said he and his dad saw coaches from Duke and Princeton at the concession stand." In his excitement, Tuna sprayed Ben with flecks of spit. "My dad told me if I get into Duke, he'll buy me any car I want, and I want a Range Rover. So, if you're me, you're pooping your pants right about now."

Ben scowled at his friend. "He's just a kid like you and me."

"He's a beast." Tuna shook his head, angling his eyes at the ground to reject any arguments.

This infuriated Ben, slicing through exhaustion and doubt. Coach Lockwood blew his whistle and pointed toward a field where players from two teams were lined up and shaking hands. "Let's go!" he shouted, and Ben and his teammates made their way over to the field. During warm-ups, Ben couldn't keep his eyes off of Heckler. He was enormous, a beast, moving quickly in tight and fast with long loping strides out in the open.

The hairs on the back of Ben's neck weren't raised as much as they had been in his talk with Tuna, but he still had a fire in his gut that made him eager to get the game started.

It came before he knew it.

Heckler won the face-off. Ben glanced back at Tuna in the goal. He stood frozen with fear, his goalies stick rigid, and its wide net protecting his face. Ben turned back, and Heckler was only two steps away. He was a giant—red shorts, red shoes, red jersey, red helmet. In that brief moment before Heckler was on him, Ben noticed the beginnings of a dark fuzzy mustache on his opponent's upper lip. Ben clenched his teeth and swung down with his long pole like a battle-ax. He blinked before the moment of impact.

His stick struck the turf. Ben grunted, and when his eyes opened, Heckler was gone. Ben spun around in time to see Heckler switch back to a right-handed grip, fake a high shot, then whip the ball with an underhand shot right in the five hole between Tuna's trembling knees.

It was only twelve seconds into the game and Maryland was already up 1–0.

Through the fog of the game, Ben heard two voices.

"Ben! What are you doing!?" That was Coach Lockwood's fearsome roar.

"C'mon, Ben! Go get him, Ben! You can do it! You got this!" That was his mom's shrill cry. Ben took a quick glance at the sidelines and saw the look of concern on his dad's face. Ben's dad never yelled at lacrosse games. He said he didn't know enough about the sport to yell anything, but he watched with intensity.

Ben made the mistake of glancing back at Tuna.

"See?" Tuna was as wide-eyed as one of the sunfish he would catch in his boathouse. "I told you!"

Ben shook his head and turned his attention to the face-off. He needed to process what had just happened and what he could do about it. He wasn't going to spend the morning being

60

some kid's doormat, no matter who the kid was. The college coaches didn't mean as much as his own pride. He was planning on a football scholarship anyway.

And he knew what he could do about it because he had attended several clinics with a coach named Rick Beardsley. Coach Beardsley was a lacrosse defensive superstar, and he coached like he had played. He was a maniac. Besides Coach Beardsley's clinics, Ben's dad had arranged for nearly a dozen one-on-one sessions with the famous coach over the course of the winter. Ben's dad believed great coaching was the key to success in sports, and Coach Lockwood was an amazing coach, but strictly for offense. But between coaches Beardsley and Lockwood, Ben got a full spectrum of offense and defense.

What Heckler did to Ben was fake to the right, then switch hands and go left. Most kids that big didn't have the stick skills to switch hands, but Heckler did. Ben remembered now what Coach Beardsley had taught him.

"You gotta chop! Chop!" he had said.

Ben could see his coach's demonic face and the blinding speed of his arms and hands as he chopped first left, then right, like some swordsman from long ago.

The whistle blew, and Heckler won the draw again. Ben got ready as he watched his opponent slash through the defensive midfielders in a blur of red, and Heckler came right at him.

When Heckler stepped to his right, Ben chopped left hard but was ready when Heckler went to his left, switching hands. Ben chopped right with all his might. Heckler spun like a top back to his right and was gone. Ben pivoted back and chased Heckler toward the goal. Ben didn't stand a chance. Heckler ran full speed across the face of the goal. Tuna moved with him, cutting off his shot until Heckler swung the stick behind his back, rifling the ball into the open side of the net, which jumped suddenly to life like a spooked bullfrog.

Only twenty-nine seconds had expired.

Coach Lockwood's hands flailed in the air. "Ben!" Coach screamed, pulling his hair so hard he nearly lifted himself off the ground. "You gotta stop that guy!"

The broiling turf beneath his cleats made Ben feel like a fire walker. With the sun beating down as harshly as his coach's anger, he mentally slipped away to the cool green water of his lake. Tuna's stick in his kidney brought Ben back with a jolt.

"You're making me look pretty bad, partner."

"You mean Heckler is making you look pretty bad." Ben's fury did nothing to cool him down.

"It's easy to blame the goalie, but he's gotta have some defense in front of him. Everyone knows that." Tuna was like a dog with a bone, so Ben walked away.

His mom was hollering at him again. He shook his head without looking, hoping that she would get his signal and stop.

"You got this, Ben! You can do it!"

No such luck.

Still, it was better than Coach yelling or Tuna complaining. The whole thing made Ben madder than a wet hornet. Things couldn't get any worse, and then Ben had an idea.

The ref was lining up the face-off. Coach Lockwood had put Charlie out there this time. Charlie wasn't nearly as big as Heckler, but he was a fighter. The whistle blew, and the battle was on, both boys grinding the heads of their sticks into the turf to get the ball. When Heckler came up with it, Ben's muscles tightened, but Charlie wasn't finished.

Quick as a cat, Charlie closed the gap between him and Heckler. Charlie slashed down on Heckler's stick with his own. The ball spilled to the turf, and Charlie had it going the other way before Heckler knew what was happening. Ben felt a cheer rise up in his throat. Charlie dodged and weaved through the Maryland defense, but when he closed in on the goal, two hefty defenders made a Charlie sandwich.

Ben's stomach sank.

Then, somehow, some way, the ball shot out of the sandwich into Luke's waiting stick. The ball no sooner hit the basket of Luke's stick than he fired it into the top-left corner of the goal. Two minutes into the game the score was 2–1. It looked like an offensive shoot-out.

But if Ben's plan worked, that would all change.

Heckler was more careful on the next face-off. When he got the ball, he cradled his stick tighter to his body, and Charlie's slashing was useless. Ben got in the same defensive stance he had in the first seconds of the game. He wanted everything to look the same, like he was some frightened chump that Heckler was going to embarrass all day long. Heckler made fools of the defending middies and bore down on Ben with a nasty smile.

Ben waited just until the instant before Heckler would make his first move. Then Ben exploded from his stance. Coach Beardsley called it offensive defense. Before Heckler knew what was happening, Ben was into him. With both hands on his long pole about three feet apart, Ben drove the stick into Heckler's chest. The unsuspecting giant flew up and dropped hard. It was a yard sale.

Ben never stopped. He followed his stick right over Heckler, planting a cleat in his arm, and scooping up the spilled ball on his way upfield. Heckler wasn't the only fast big guy. Ben poured on the speed and raced up the sideline, outrunning Maryland's midfielders before veering into its defense.

Ben put a move on the first defender that might have broken the kid's ankles. When two more defenders came at Ben from either side, he showed off his smarts by unloading a pass to his wide-open buddy Reed, who didn't waste a moment before firing the ball in the lower-left corner for a goal.

The Maryland coach lost his mind. He jumped up and down screaming at the referees for a penalty against Ben. As Ben jogged back toward his position, the Maryland coach, dressed in all red with a dark beard, dashed out onto the field and collared Ben before he knew what was happening.

"You need to flag this kid and eject him before I do!" the coach bellowed.

Ben struggled to get free.

A ref got right up in the coach's face. "That was a clean stick check, Coach! Now you get off the field or you're gone!"

"Clean?" The coach pointed toward the sideline where an adult examined Heckler's arm. "He stomped on my guy and he's done for the day. My best guy!"

"Off!" The ref waved his flag. "I say it again and you're gone, Coach. I mean it. The hit was clean, and he in no way stomped your guy. Your guy was down, and this young man ran over the top of him. There was nothing dirty about it."

The coach raised his hands, letting go of Ben's collar, turned, and walked away grumbling. Ben was so shaken up he could only mutter a brief thanks to the ref.

"It was all clean," said the ref once more.

Ben turned and saw his dad on the opposite sideline out of his chair, being held back by his mom, who held one arm with two hands.

The Maryland team was still tough, even without Heckler, but Orange Crush gained a one-point lead and held on to it until the final horn. They mobbed Tuna, who had an outstanding day.

"I knew we could take these guys," Tuna said to Ben as they marched off the field after shaking hands with a subdued Maryland team minus their Goliath, Heckler.

"Yeah, you called it." Ben had to look straight ahead in order not to grin.

On the sideline, Ben hugged his parents despite being drenched in sweat. He refueled with a couple Powerades before they hit the road.

"What a nice way to end the season," said Ben's mom.

"You should've led me bussed dat coach in da mouff." Ben's dad muttered some other observations under his breath.

Ben's mom frowned. "And that wouldn't have been a nice way to end the season."

Ben's dad sighed as they passed through the toll booth and onto the Pennsylvania Turnpike. "Congradulashuns, Ben. You played awesome. Now less go ged a championshib in fudball dis season."

The summer had passed for Ben like all the summers before, in a blink of sun and water and throwing the football. Ben enjoyed himself, but the weight of his dad's condition hung over everything. Over the weeks, things had progressed more quickly than Ben had thought they would. Judging from the secret looks between them, Ben knew his brothers were surprised too. His dad now walked with a cane and couldn't go very far. He no longer took his daily three-mile walk with Ben's mom, and his speech was becoming harder and harder to understand.

Ben hadn't attended any more sleepovers since the night of the stinky eggs. He always had a ready excuse with his brothers, who, in all truth, did take him to a lot of movies during the summer. That's why he had his friends over now. Ben and his teammates were having a last summer barbecue/sleepover, complete with firepit s'mores, before practice started the next day. What he didn't mind was having sleepovers at his house, and ending the summer with one at his place would make his friends forget about all the times he'd said no.

"So this is it." Tuna poked at the fire with a stick, sending a cascade of orange sparks from the firepit into the cool night air.

"You make it sound like prison or something." Finn shivered and buttoned his jean jacket before putting another marshmallow on his stick.

Tuna groaned. "Prison? Prison would be a holiday compared to bear crawls and cross-fields."

"What about the pit drill and Oklahomas and sharks and minnows?" Malik took a golden-brown marshmallow off his stick and popped it into his mouth, so the rest of his words were a sticky mess. "Ith wots mo fun den Pop Warner en Auburn. Dem boys craythy."

Ben's face warmed with pride. They practiced hard, but one thing his dad tried to do was make practices as fun as possible. Ben thought about how he had worried that his dad wouldn't even be able to coach. He smiled to himself, because despite all the challenges, his dad insisted that he would be the coach of Ben's team. Ben dug into his pocket and removed his phone. The calendar didn't have many entries, but tomorrow, August 4, and every day thereafter until October 13, was marked FOOTBALL. The sight tugged his lips into a bigger smile. He had worked hard with his brothers. He knew all the plays, and his arm was in great shape.

After a while, the fire died down and even Woody began to yawn.

"Big day tomorrow." Finn stood up and tossed his stick in the remains of the fire. "I need to get some sleep."

One by one they stood, copying Finn and tossing their own sticks in the fire so that the flames revived for a final moment. They trudged up the steps of the concrete pathway and deck, breathing heavily by the time they reached the top, and entered the house through the kitchen. Ben's dad was sitting at the kitchen table drinking yellow cans of lemon seltzer with Ben's brother Rich and Coach Sindoni, the high school varsity coach. Ben's teammates were speechless, even Woody.

"Wuth up, boys?"

Ben looked at his friends to see if any of them noticed his dad's slight slur. They were too busy staring in awe at Coach Sindoni, who was a celebrity in their small town. He was the man who'd delivered the high school varsity team the first state championship in its entire history.

Coach Sindoni scowled at the handful of boys. "Coach Redd is talking to you guys."

"Oh, hey, Coach Redd. We just had a firepit down at the lake. Marshmallows and sodas, you know, and now we're turning in because Tuna's worried about bear crawls." Woody paused to catch his breath and drew a dirty look from Tuna.

"Tuna thould worry abow bear crawls. We need him to play both ways iss year, so he needs ta be in thape." Ben's dad raised the seltzer can to toast Tuna, then to take a drink, but the can slipped from his fingers and crashed onto the table spraying seltzer everywhere.

"Whoa!" cried Coach Sindoni as he leaped back from the table, soaking wet. "No, don't worry, don't worry. I'll get a towel."

Ben could see the flush in his dad's cheeks. He looked at his friends, who were staring at what just happened. Ben circled the table and grabbed a towel himself. He handed one to the coach, and together they mopped up the mess. Ben's dad sat looking grimly at the hands that had betrayed him. Ben's teammates had stopped staring and were now shifting uncomfortably.

"Okay, umm, we're going to head down to the basement." Ben kissed his dad and said good night before turning to his friends. "Come on, guys."

They went downstairs, where five flat-screen TVs lined one wall and signed jerseys of famous NFL players framed behind glass hung shoulder to shoulder on the rest of the wall space. Two rows of thick couches and chairs faced the TVs. Everyone signed in on the Xbox consoles, and they played *Fortnight* until Ben's dad shouted lights-out from the top of the stairs.

The five friends made their way through the weight room to a bunk room with eight beds. Two boys went up, and three, including Ben, stayed in the bottom bunks. There was the usual chatter before things quieted down. Tuna slept next to Ben. He shifted, and the bedframe groaned. Beyond him Woody breathed like a four-hundred-pound man.

Ben stared up at the wood frame above, the sounds of sleep all around him. Alone in the darkness, he wondered how his dad could coach if he could barely speak or hold a can of soda. He wasn't sure how the team would react, either. But then Ben took it one step further, and he wondered whether or not his dad would even make it through their season.

The August sun beat down upon the grass and the players in their shoulder pads and stretchy gold nylon pants that matched their helmets. The narrow parking lot beside the practice field was packed. Many of the parents had set up folding chairs on the side of the field. Ben was throwing go routes to any receivers who chose to do so. No one had a better feel for the long bombs than Finn. Ben's dad was huddled up with his brothers and three other assistant coaches: Fergy, who played on Rich's high school championship team; Mr. Bennett, whose son Torin was another favorite target of Ben's; and Scotty, a bulky college teammate of Raymond's who was also good friends with Rich.

When a rusty white pickup truck with a broken muffler rumbled into the lot spewing great clouds of blue smoke, Ben watched from the corner of his eye while he continued to throw. The truck pulled right up in front of the fire hydrant and a scruffy man with a ragged beard, dirty jeans, and a torn faded red T-shirt hopped out with a girl Ben's age.

The man questioned someone's dad sitting in a lawn chair. The dad pointed at the group of coaches, and the man made a beeline for Ben's dad with the girl in tow. She had blonde hair, like her dad, only hers was braided into two long pigtails. Her elfin face was smudged with dirt; she looked like a pretty farm girl. Hoping to hear their conversation, Ben edged closer to the group of coaches, telling his teammates that he wanted to work on some throws from a rollout position.

"Evenin', Coach." The man touched the bill of his dirty cap. His hair fell straight to his collar. "Jed Labourdette."

"Hi." Ben's dad wore a smile, as he always did with strangers, although he remained in his director's chair while he shook the man's hand.

"So, sorry we missed the sign-ups, but I was busy gettin' my beans in. My wife signed Thea Jean up in Auburn, but when we got there, they said no girls. They said they got cheerleading for girls." The man laughed in a sour way.

"My wife looked at y'all's website, and it said girls are welcome to play, so here she is." Thea popped out from behind her dad's back and said, "Hi!"

Ben watched his dad's jaw drop only to recover immediately with a smile. "Oh, umm, sure. Coach Benned will ged her some quipmend, an she ken join ride in if she wands."

"That'll suit her just fine, won't it, Thea Jean?"

Thea Jean offered a shy smile but nodded her head.

"She loves football. Plays with her brothers in the yard every chance she gets. She may not look like much, but she's tough as

73

an old boot." Thea Jean's dad put a hand on her head.

Coach Bennett said, "Come with me. We'll get you signed up and get Thea some equipment."

Ben watched the three of them heading for the equipment trailer that rested on the grass between their practice field and the high school baseball diamond. He turned and saw that everyone else was watching too, and not just his teammates, but the coaches and parents as well.

Woody tossed a ball to Ben, breaking his trance. "Well, there goes the championship. I can only imagine what Penn Yan is gonna think when they see we've got a girl on the team."

The whistle blew, and they had a five-minute water break after an agility period that left everyone huffing and drenched in sweat.

Tuna flopped on the grass. "I swear I'm gonna puke, and we barely even started. Brother, can you get your dad to ease up? On the big guys anyway?"

Ben took a swig of water and tossed Tuna his own water bottle. "My dad doesn't make up the agility drills. That's Raymond. And if I say anything to him, he'll just make it harder."

"Whaddaya say, whaddaya know!"

"Hey, Woody." Ben bumped fists with his friend.

"Well?" Woody waved a hand toward the field. "Whaddaya know!"

"Oh, we're doing Oklahoma drills, I think."

"Now you're talking." Woody leaned into Ben and lightly bumped heads. "Crackin' heads. Let's get you, me, and Malik. We will crush everyone and anyone."

"Hey, what about the big Tuna?" Tuna hoisted himself off the ground.

Ben wasn't saying anything. He wasn't going to be the one to hurt the big guy's feelings.

"Oh, Tuna, didn't see you lying there in the grass. Yeah, sorry but we already got three," said Woody.

Tuna looked around. "You don't have Malik."

"The whole thing was Malik's idea in the first place. Sorry, Big Tuna. Next time, maybe." Woody turned and gave Ben a wink.

Ben didn't feel comfortable. He didn't like to hurt anyone's feelings, especially Tuna, who he knew was as sensitive as he was big. Before Ben could do anything about it, the whistle blew. Everyone dropped his water bottle and raced toward the cluster of coaches on the far side of the field.

Foam blocking dummies made up three narrow ten-yard lanes. Everyone was grouped into threes either by their own doing or the coaches. The Oklahoma drill was a violent mini football game that put two players of the three-man teams on the line of scrimmage. If the team was on offense, then the third man was the ball carrier. If the team was on defense, the third man was a linebacker. After each play, the players would change positions. The offense had four plays to go ten yards for a touchdown. If they scored, or failed, the other team took over on offense.

Ben knew what Woody was doing. He and Malik were fast

skill players who were also big, so anyone teamed up with the two of them stood a good chance of crushing their opponents. And Woody knew that. Somehow out of the scrum of thirty-one players emerged ten teams of three and one extra kid, Jack Harding, a skinny fifth grader who acted like he didn't want to be there.

"Look who we got!" Woody giggled gleefully, pointing to none other than Tuna, the starting left guard named Rohan Schmitt, and Thea, the girl.

Woody was snorting and pawing at the earth when Coach Rich came over to their group with Jack Harding in tow and said, "Ben, you're coming with me. Coach Bennett will take this group and Jack will take your place."

Ben knew better but couldn't keep himself from asking, "But why?"

Rich's face turned dark. "Because I'm the coach, that's why. Do you want to win a championship, or play second fiddle to Penn Yan like last year? Well?"

Ben looked at the grass. "Championship."

"That's right. You're our quarterback. You don't block and tackle, so this drill is a good time for you and me to go over your footwork. Now, let's go!" Rich turned and jogged away toward the opposite end zone.

Ben glanced at Woody's outraged face and shrugged before taking off after his brother.

The sounds of pads popping and helmets cracking filled Ben's ears.

"Did you hear what I said?" Rich's voice cut through the sweet sounds of contact.

"Uh, yeah, a five-step drop," Ben answered.

"Well, do it!"

Ben held the ball out in front of him, pretending to take a snap. "Blue twenty-seven, blue twenty-seven, set . . . go!"

Ben cranked his hips, sprung backward for five steps, and set his body to throw.

"Stand tall, and I want the ball pointing down!" Rich wasn't much of a screamer, but the angry tone of his voice could melt glass. "If you're not going to do the little things right in life, then you can't succeed. Not just in football. I'm talking about life."

"Whadda heck are you guys doin'?"

Ben and Rich both spun around. Their dad had abandoned the sturdy aluminum director's chair that their mom got because it was hard for him to stand for any length of time. He was struggling along, with his cane biting small divots out of the grass.

Rich straightened his back. "Ben and I are polishing off his five-step drops. He doesn't need to do Oklahoma drills; he doesn't play defense and he doesn't block."

Ben's dad scowled at his middle son. "You kin do diss when we do deem defenz. You doen jus dezide yer gonna do drills when we god Oklahomas."

"I'm the offensive coordinator."

Ben held his breath.

His dad began to boil. "Am I nod da head coach anymore?"

"Dad, there's no reason for him to do that drill. He doesn't need to bang his head."

"You sound like your mudder." Ben's dad waved a dismissive hand.

"She happens to be right." Rich said it like an apology so their dad almost couldn't take offense.

"Dere's a big difference bedween whad dee's guys are doin' an da NFL."

"Why even take a chance, Dad? He's got things he needs to work on with me, anyway."

Their dad opened his mouth to speak but instead waved another dismissive hand, turned, and walked away.

Ben heard what his brother said, but his dad had to be right. Even when he played in the NFL one day, he'd be a quarterback, not a grunt down in the trenches like his dad, banging his head on every play. The NFL protected its quarterbacks.

"He is a mule," Rich said when their dad was far enough that he couldn't hear.

"He's right, Rich."

Rich scowled at him. He looked just like their dad. "You have no clue, Bo."

Ben shook his head and started to walk away, following in his father's footsteps, determined to be a part of the Oklahoma drills.

"Hey!" Rich shouted. "You walk away, you're done playing quarterback for me."

It was at the very next water break when Woody jumped all over Ben.

"What in the Wild West was that?" Woody said loudly enough so that everyone turned his head.

"What was what?" Ben shrugged like he hadn't a clue.

"Leaving me and Malik hanging in Oklahomas!" Woody wore a look of disbelief. "Harding melted like ice cream in a skillet. We got mauled is what, while you were practicing ballet or something."

"I do what the coaches tell me to do." Ben felt his cheeks burning.

"That's some home cookin' is what that is." The bigger the audience, the bigger Woody's mouth was. "Is that some home cookin' or what, Malik?"

"Chill, Woody. You missed a boatload of blocks and about

as many tackles as Jack did." Malik turned his back and took a slug of orange Gatorade.

That seemed to diffuse the situation, and Woody stomped away, mumbling.

Ben edged over to where Malik was polishing off his drink. "Hey, thanks for that. I think you're the only one who's ever left Woody speechless."

"I don't play that home-cookin' junk. We're lucky to have your dad and your brothers, and we're lucky to have you. They treat you like everyone else. If anything, they're harder on you. There's no home cookin', and he knows it. He's being a chump." Malik scowled in Woody's direction. "I'll tell you why he's really mad. That girl lit him up like a Christmas tree."

"She did?"

Malik rubbed his arm. "Hits like a mule. She blocked Woody into the dirt. And when she tackled him? My man was airborne."

"Really?" Ben spotted Thea sitting on the grass at the edge of the crowd all by herself. "When her dad said that she was as tough as an old boot, I thought it was a joke."

"It's no joke, Brother. It's no joke."

Ben marched right over to Thea and extended his hand. "I'm Ben Redd."

Thea was even prettier up close. She had bright green eyes and a slightly upturned nose. She reminded Ben of a pixie, but she only squinted at his hand. "So?"

Ben dropped his hand. "I'm the quarterback."

"Aren't you lucky." Her mouth was flat as a hatchet cut.

Ben shrugged and walked away.

Tuna intercepted him. "What were you doing with her?"

"Just welcoming her to the team. I heard she gave Woody a mouthful of those braids."

Tuna chuckled. "Shoulda seen Woody's face."

"He's trying to blame it all on me. 'Home cookin',' he says. He should get half the shade my brother throws on me. See how he likes it."

Tuna frowned. "What's that mean, home cookin'?"

"Like, my brother favors me and doesn't want me to get hurt. I want to do Oklahomas and I want to do tackling drills and play defense. When you guys are doing that, he has all these quarterback drills he wants me to do." Ben didn't want to sound like he was whining, but he also wouldn't mind some sympathy from his friend.

Tuna shrugged. "You're Q1. Anybody who doesn't get that shouldn't be playing football. You're the man, Ben. Not because your dad played in the NFL, or your brothers were stars here, but because without you, I don't know how many games we'd win. We sure aren't gonna beat Penn Yan without you."

Ben put a hand on Tuna's shoulder pad and gave him a painful smile just as the whistle blew.

Practice ended the way Ben liked. He got to prove to the team what Tuna already believed to be true in a live scrimmage. Because everyone played, Ben's dad encouraged his coaching sons to have twenty-two starters. While they didn't quite need twenty-two, they had only a handful of kids who started both ways. That meant that they could have a pretty robust live scrimmage that pitted Raymond's defensive mind against Rich's offensive mind.

Since they played a no-huddle spread offense, Rich insisted they practice that way. So he had Jake Moreland 's dad—Jake was their starting right guard, a killer—hold up huge poster-sized cards covered with all kinds of images. Only the team knew what image on each board meant, giving them the number of the play they would run. The idea came from Rich's days playing quarterback at University of Central Florida and then Syracuse University.

When Ben lined up in a shotgun position four yards behind the center, he and the whole offense had seen the card Mr. Moreland had held up with his back to the defense. Among the images of random things like fire trucks, animals, and cartoon characters were sports stars. Each card had one sports star, and the jersey number of that star was the number of the play. The player on the card had been Michael Vick, number seven, the bubble screen. It was a quick pass to Malik with two blockers, Torin and Woody, in front of him.

Ben looked over his offense to make sure everyone was in the correct place. He then surveyed the defense and paused a moment. Playing free safety was Thea, with her two braids draped down the front of her shoulder pads. Was Raymond really going to start a girl?

"Ben! You can't daydream!" Rich's shout jolted Ben into action.

"Orange ten! Orange ten! Set . . . go!"

The center snapped the ball over Ben's head. He stayed calm, scrambling to retrieve the ball and zip it to Malik. The play should still have worked. Malik was a bruiser, and he had two able blockers in front of him. Still, Thea came flying like a missile, split the blockers, and blew up Malik at the line of scrimmage for no gain.

"Woody!" Rich howled. "That's your block. C'mon, buddy. That's a block I know you can make."

"I thought I had strong safety, Coach." Woody clenched his fists.

"But if the free safety is in your face, you can't just let him go by you and destroy your runner, can you?" Rich put his arm around Woody's shoulders.

Woody wore a look of horror. "No, Coach."

Rich raised his voice again. "Look, you'll probably see very few safety blitzes in this league. Coach Raymond likes to show off sometimes."

Raymond cupped his hands around his mouth. "That wasn't a blitz, Coach! Your quarterback mishandled the snap, and my free safety read it and blew up the play!"

Rich turned his back without comment, but to Ben he said, "C'mon, let's stick one in his end zone."

Rich then turned to the center, Rohan Schmitt, a tall, tough, lanky lineman with long blond hair. "Ro, I yelled at Ben because he's the quarterback, but I really need you to get that snap down, buddy, okay?"

Ro hung his head and nodded. He was an excellent lineman but new to the position of center.

Rich whispered to Jake's dad, and he held up the board with Falcons All-Pro quarterback Matt Ryan's picture among the other images. Matt Ryan wore number two. Two was a hitch-and-go play, the downtown special between Ben and his lightning-fast buddy Finn.

"Oh yeah." Ben clapped his hands together with excitement.

He surveyed his offense. Everyone was in his place, and he couldn't help but grin at Finn when he caught his eye. He glanced at the defense, scowling at Thea, who was lined up shallow in center field, the perfect position for being burned on a deep pass. Ben's voice rose with delight. "Green seventeen! Green seventeen! Set . . . go!"

The snap this time skittered across the grass. Ben snatched it up and pump-faked to Finn on a hitch, which was a one-yard pass route. The cornerback charged at Finn, biting on the fake. From the corner of his eye, Ben saw the middle linebackers tearing through his line on a blitz. He took a jab step to the right, then spun back to his left and took off for the sideline.

Finn was thirty yards downfield with the cornerback trailing hopelessly far behind. The girl was in hot pursuit but could never close the gap. It wouldn't be an easy pass for Ben to make, though. He was racing to his left, so he'd have to crank his hips completely around before launching the ball. Now he was glad that Rich had made him do just that hundreds, maybe thousands of times over the summer.

He cranked his hips and let it fly. There was something beautiful, pure, and clean about a perfectly thrown go route. Ben swelled with pride, admiring the spin as the ball arced and began its descent toward Finn's outstretched hands. Finn caught it in stride. Ben pumped a fist in the air, but Thea had changed her angle, not to break up the pass, but to cut Finn off at the goal line. It would be close, but Ben's money was on Finn.

Ben clenched his teeth. No, Thea would never make it. Even if she hit Finn, which she might, she'd be tackling him into the end zone.

He had to be right!

Ben was right. Thea couldn't make the tackle.

But what she could do, and what she *did* do, was punch the ball out of the crook of Finn's arm to send it flying through the back of the end zone.

Raymond was going absolutely bananas.

He ran over to Thea, and after patting her on the back about two dozen times, he hollered, "That's a touchback! No touchdown! Our ball on the twenty-yard line going the other way, baby!"

Ben didn't know if Raymond made a flourish with his arms and dramatically pointed his finger toward the opposite end zone because he was excited or because he wanted to rub Rich's nose in it. Either way, Rich was furious. He called the offense into a loose huddle.

When he spoke, though, his voice was measured. "Ro,

you're killing me, buddy. You got to get the ball to the quarter-back. We can't have every play off by a few seconds because of a bad snap, not in this offense anyway."

Ro hung his head.

"Did you practice over the summer, Ro?" Rich's voice was soft and pleasant.

Ro nodded and raised his chin.

Rich raised his eyebrows. "Every day, Ro? Every single day like we talked about?"

Ro dropped his head again, and it seemed like someone had severed his spine.

"Uh-huh." Rich nodded and turned his attention to Finn. "Finn, you made a fantastic catch, just beautiful, but we work on what every day?"

Finn's modest smile melted. "Ball security, Coach."

"Ball security." Rich looked around the huddle. "Guys, we can't win the big games if we don't do the little things right. Right? Okay, who remembers what play number three is? Damon?"

Ben knew that Damon was one of Rich's favorite players. He was super polite and super talented, as skinny as Finn, but taller and not quite as fast.

He was the strong side wide receiver, so of course he knew what play number three was. "Reverse, Coach."

"Reverse. And what if I signal this to you and Ben?" Rich crossed his arms, making an X.

"That means Ben keeps it, but I gotta fake like it's the reverse anyway."

Rich patted Damon's helmet. "That's right, buddy. You

gotta sell it. Okay, play number three, run it."

Ben bubbled with excitement. Pride lifted him like a hot-air balloon. Rich wanted to put one on Raymond's defense, and the way he chose to do it was with Ben.

"Yellow ten! Yellow ten! Set . . . go!"

The snap went wild again, this time high and to the right. Ben leaped up like a goalkeeper, snatched the ball, hauled it in, and took off for the sideline. Damon took one jab step forward, then hit reverse, and ran in an arc that intersected with Ben's rollout. Ben stuck the ball in his gut, and Damon bent slightly while pretending to cradle the ball in his arms. Damon took off like a flash, and Ben pinned the ball to his right hip, slowed down, and looked back at Damon like a spectator.

The cornerback and the strong safety hollered, "Reverse! Reverse!" at the top of their lungs, and the word spread throughout the defense like a virus.

Ben let them all turn and run before kicking it back into high gear. He was ten yards down the sideline before Thea sniffed something fishy, stopped suddenly, did a reverse of her own, and took off like a cheetah.

Ben felt something like rocket fuel flood his legs. His stride felt ten feet long, and only his toes seemed to barely nick the grass. Still, Thea flew at a speed and an angle that would cut him off five or ten yards from the end zone.

In that instant before impact, Ben realized his reputation was on the line, and with that, maybe the entire season. The rest of the team counted on him to be outstanding.

How would it look to all his friends, his brothers, his dad if he was denied the end zone by a girl?

27

When they collided, Thea crashed into Ben's knees with a terrible force.

This wasn't Ben's first rodeo, though. Just as she smashed into his knees, Ben thrusted a hand down onto her helmet, driving her head into the dirt with a textbook stiff arm. In the same motion, he regained his legs and kept going until he reached the end zone.

Ben struggled to control himself. He looked over at his dad sitting high up in his director's chair with his eyes glued to Ben and a flat line for a mouth. What Ben wanted to do was spike the ball in the end zone, but that would never do. He had spiked the ball in practice last summer, and his dad warned the whole team that anyone who spiked the ball or did anything silly in the end zone, or anywhere else on the field, would immediately find themselves on the bench. So instead

Ben jogged back to where his offensive teammates were slapping high fives. He handed the ball to Coach Bennett while Thea walked back to her spot-on defense with fire in her eyes.

Tuna was the first to slap him on the back. "Awesome stiff arm, my man."

"You put that girl DOWN!" Woody's eyes were big as saucers, and his smile was a mile wide. "Whaddaya say, whaddaya know!"

The entire offense was grinning, even mild-mannered Finn.

"Nice play, Bo." Rich wasn't as excited as Ben's teammates, but any praise from him was big. "All right, you guys, that was one good play, and, Ro, you're killing me with those snaps. C'mon, buddy, get it going."

They ran the next play, the reverse again, but this time Damon kept it. He gained ten yards before Thea knocked him down like a bowling pin. Damon stayed down, moaning and thrashing and holding his right knee. Rich and Raymond both ran over to him. His teammates crowded around but gave the coaches plenty of room.

Ben pushed through the pack to the inside of the circle. Damon's moaning got louder and louder. Ben saw Thea standing on the opposite side of the circle with a look of scorn on her face. Ben saw red. He was wild.

He dashed across the circle. "You idiot! He's one of our best players, and you just cheap-shotted him!"

Thea snorted at him, and Ben pushed her arm. She stumbled back and fell to the ground.

"Hey!" she shouted, popping up and kicking him in the shin.

Ben howled. "What the—!"

"Enough! Both of you!" Rich jumped up and separated the two of them. His face was twisted and bright red. "Laps around this field until I say stop! Now start running!"

Ben limped his way to the sideline, hoping for some sympathy from his brother or better yet, his father. Thea darted past him like a rabbit. Ben immediately abandoned his limp and took off after her.

They ran and ran, taking turns passing each other and muttering insults as they did.

Solomon Voytovich, an athletic fifth grader, replaced Ben as quarterback for the next couple of plays. And he was doing quite well. It burned Ben to see Rich high-fiving and then putting his arm around Sol after a big play. It was as if the team didn't really need or even miss him. Meanwhile, he was running out of gas. Only his pride, and the sight of those two blonde braids bouncing in front of him, kept him from collapsing.

After a few times around the field, Ben had stopped counting the laps. Pride or no, he couldn't do more than a sad jog. His only comfort was the sight of Thea stumbling along at a pace that allowed him to close the most recent gap between them. Her braids had definitely lost their bounce. They lay dead as roadkill against the back of her shoulder pads.

His shin throbbed, but he was determined not to give her the satisfaction of knowing that she'd hurt him in the least. As he caught up to her, he gasped for the air to insult her, but only had breath enough to stay on his feet.

She, on the other hand, seemed to still have some reserves. "Your brother's . . . a jerk."

"Good . . . Then . . . you . . . can . . . quit." Ben wouldn't have had the energy to respond if she'd bad-mouthed him, but his brother?

She dropped back behind him for a few paces before she gasped and said, "I never . . . quit. . . ."

"All right, you two!" Rich shouted with his hands cupped around his mouth. "Take five and come back as teammates, or you can both run till the end of practice!"

Ben stopped running. He put one foot in front of the other so as not to collapse.

"Teammates?" Her stupid laugh reminded him of a hyena.

Ben muttered so only she could hear. "Never."

Ben and Thea spent their water break glaring at each other for the first minute, then pretending the other one didn't even exist. At about the five-minute mark, Thea broke the silence.

"If you can see straight, you'll notice that there's nothing wrong with one of your best players."

It was true. Damon was clearly okay and running a deep route at that moment going full speed. That didn't make what she did okay, but how could he argue that without her cutting him off with some nasty comment? He knew her tongue was as sharp as it was quick.

Ben ignored her, caught his breath, and then jogged over to the offensive side of the field. "Damon, what the heck?"

His friend spun around with a look of surprise, then shrugged. "I thought I was done, Ben. I swear, my knee opened up like a door hinge. It hurt so bad, but then your dad called a doctor friend who lives in town. He was at Doug's Fish Fry, and he came right over and said I was okay. Then your dad said to try and walk it off, and it worked! He said he's had that happen to him, so . . ."

"Yeah, well . . ."

"Hey, Ben, I'm sorry you got in trouble."

Ben punched Damon's shoulder pad. "No problem, Damon. Just make sure you keep catching my passes, even the bad ones."

Damon gave him a big smile, and they bumped fists.

Ben buckled his helmet and approached his brother. "I'm ready, Rich."

Rich glanced at him before huddling up the offense to give Sol some instructions on the next play. Sol barked out the cadence, and the snap went over his head. Ben bit back a grin. It was a bad, high snap, but one which Ben would have managed to get because he was much taller than Sol.

The ball sailed seven yards over Sol's head. The defense poured through the gaps. Sol sensed them coming, tried to scoop up the ball, bumbled it, and got swamped by a wave of defenders. Big Luke Logan came up with the ball from beneath the pile. Raymond sprinted from the defensive secondary to the pile deep behind the line.

He hugged Luke, then made a big show of pointing the opposite way and yelling, "First down!"

Ben's dad shouted from his perch, "Coach! You godda ged yer snap fixed!"

Rich scowled, looked like he was going to shout something back to their dad, but thought better of it, and kicked the grass instead. "Okay, Sol, that wasn't your fault. You did a great job in there, but I'm putting Ben back in now."

Ben only got to run six more plays before his father blew the whistle, ending their team period. His dad was up out of his chair now and talking quietly to Raymond.

Raymond nodded and turned to the team, blowing his whistle. "Okay, five teams, the same group you did Oklahomas with! Half on one sideline, half on the other for relay races!"

The players actually cheered, and Ben joined them. It was a fun, competitive way of getting in shape, much better than just everyone on the line to run sprints. Everyone but the winners had to do ten push-ups after the race. Rich told Ben to join Woody's group.

Woody raised his hand. "Should we each run one less, Coach, to make it even with the other teams?"

"No, Woody, you all will have to really turn it on. But don't worry, you're fast, and you've got a pretty fast group with you."

Woody hung his head, kicked some grass, and muttered something no one could hear.

Rich stepped back into the middle of the field and raised his voice so everyone could hear. "So the anchor of our offensive line had a great idea. Instead of running this relay race, we're going to bear crawl!"

As the moans and groans erupted, Rich blew his whistle, signaling a start to the race.

Ben found himself behind Thea. He fought the urge to push her again, especially for what she said about Rich. Instead, he focused on cheering on his other teammates. Rich was right— with him, Woody, and Malik, they could make up the lost time by having an extra player to make it down and back twice.

Their team cheered wildly for each other until Thea went. No one said a word. Despite the lack of encouragement, she took off like a gazelle, almost springing off the grass on all fours. She left her competition far behind.

"Wow," said Malik.

"That's trash. My guy put that girl down. Twice!" Woody was glowing.

"Yeah, but she's fast, and she hits like a hammer." Malik got down on all fours, ready to go.

"Yeah, my baby sister's pink Playskool hammer," Woody said, but not until Malik was snorting and tearing up grass halfway across the field.

Without warning, Woody grabbed Ben's jersey and gave him a great tug. "Look look look look look!" Woody laughed like a crazy man. "Tuna! Go, Tuna! Go!"

Ben spun around. Tuna was at midfield on all fours, fertilizing the grass. Spraying through his face mask were what seemed to be several chewed-up chili dogs. He made horrible retching sounds that, combined with the sight of the hot dog chunks, caused Ben's own stomach to lurch.

"Woody, get ready!" Ben shoved him toward the sideline. "You're up!"

Jack Harding crawled slowly over the line, and Woody launched himself like a missile across the field. With Tuna distracting nearly the entire team, and the speed of Ben, Malik, Woody, and even Thea, Ben's team won by a shoelace. There was none of the normal celebration, though, because Thea was the one who brought the victory home by beating a rabbit-quick Sol Voytovich.

"All right!" Raymond shouted. "Everyone but team two get down and give me ten good ones! If they're not good, your whole team will do them over again!"

Ben, Woody, Malik, and the rest of the guys, even Jack Harding, all celebrated with high fives and fist bumps. Thea stood off to the side with a look of scorn. She had her arms crossed, and she actually spit in their direction before staring at Ben until he blinked and looked away.

With the push-ups complete, Rich blew his whistle and shouted, "Everyone on Coach!"

Rich turned toward their dad and broke into a run. Everyone else followed until the whole team, players and coaches alike, stood in a crowded semicircle around Ben's dad in his director's chair.

"Dake a knee guys, dake a knee."

Ben secretly looked around, examining the sweaty faces of his teammates for signs of snickering or bitten-back smiles. He felt a flood of relief when he saw none, but when he tuned back into what his dad was saying, he couldn't believe his ears.

"When someone full of talent works that hard, it just stands out, so bravo to you, young lady."

Ben stuck a finger in his sweaty ear and gave it a fierce wiggle. Was his dad seriously praising Thea as a role model for the whole team to follow?

Yes, he was.

The other thing Ben realized was that he understood every word his dad was saying. The words to Ben were crystal clear, even though to others he knew they sounded mushy. "Okay, now, Ro, you know we all love you and you're one of our best blockers, but we can't play a spread offense without a center who can get it to the quarterback every play. So let's get you back to left guard and find someone that can do what we need to win."

Ben's dad's smile ended. "So who thinks they can snap the

ball? Anyone? And don't raise your hand unless you're willing to do a lot of extra work with Ben and Sol."

Like the rest of his teammates, Ben looked around to see who would volunteer. Tuna's hand shot up, and Ben liked that. Ro could go to tackle instead of guard, and Ben would have his buddy to rely on. Extra work would be easy. They could work together in the morning and then go WaveRunning.

The fact that Tuna was volunteering kept everyone else's hand down. He was not only their best lineman, but one of Ben's best friends.

"Tuna? That's great. Anyone else?" Ben's dad looked over his team. "Thea? Great! I like it. Nothing breeds excellence like competition."

Ben's head swung around like the rest of them. The skinny girl with the turned-up nose and blonde braids stared at the boys' faces defiantly with her hand held high.

Ben hadn't realized Woody was beside him until he felt a whisper in his ear. "I know how to fix this situation."

On their drive home, Ben's dad struggled making the turns in his mom's big Ford SUV. Raymond, who was in the front seat, turned and gave a quick knowing look to Rich, who sat behind their dad. Ben knew what they were thinking, that their dad probably should think about not driving anymore. But they all stayed silent.

"So, Bo, what did you think of that little Thea? Tough kid, right? How's your shin?" Their dad glanced at him in the rearview mirror and chuckled.

Ben scowled.

They all laughed at that, and Rich grabbed the back of his neck and gave him a loving shake. Ben squirmed free from his grip and flashed a hateful glare.

Rich just smiled. "Well, what'd you think was gonna happen? You poke a rattlesnake, you're gonna get bit."

Raymond and their dad boiled his blood with a new round of laughter. Rich quickly joined in. He loved them, but when they did this to him, he wanted to scream. Instead, he kept quiet, as always.

After their laughter had subsided, there was a minute of silence before his dad said, "Bo, you di a gray job. You frew some really nice passes an you di a gray job fieldin some crummy snaps."

"Hopefully Tuna can fix that." Ben knew what Rich's reply was going to be before he said it.

"Or maybe Thea." Rich's tone was serious.

Ben bit his lip but couldn't help himself from speaking up this time. "She's a little thin to play on the line, isn't she?"

"Did you see her hit?" Raymond's voice was full of admiration. "She's fearless."

"She leads with her head." Ben didn't want to sound whiny, so he said, "She could break her neck."

Ben's dad looked at him in the rearview mirror again before addressing his oldest son. "Ben's right. Raymond, you gotta get her head up. She'll hurt someone, maybe herself."

"Yeah, I talked to her already. She said that's the way her brothers taught her."

"Brothers?" Rich said.

"The dad said they play in their yard," said Ben's dad.

"What's their last name, Dad? Where are they from?" Rich asked.

"Uhh, Labourdette. From Auburn. Dad's a farmer."

"Labourdette? The Labourdette twins?" Rich said.

"You know them?" Raymond asked.

"I know *of* them," Rich said. "They're a lot of the reason Auburn won a state title last year. And they both got full rides to Notre Dame next year. Both inside linebackers. They're animals."

Rich knew about full rides. He'd gotten one from University of Central Florida, an all-expenses paid scholarship.

Their dad chuckled and shook his head. "No wonder her father said she's tough as a . . . tough as a . . ."

"An old boot," said Ben.

"That's it. An old boot. She's tough as an old boot, and he wasn't kidding. Hahaha!"

"And that's why she's not too skinny to play on the line," said Raymond. "You know, you should have her over to the house tomorrow before practice and work with her a little on her snaps."

"What?"

Ben couldn't believe what was happening.

They pulled into their garage. Ben was in a daze when he got out and started for the door. He was reaching for the handle when he heard an enormous thud behind him.

"Dad!" Rich shouted.

Ben spun around.

Their dad lay facedown on the concrete floor.

He wasn't moving.

Ben stood frozen while his two brothers lifted their father up off the concrete garage floor. Blood gushed from his nose, spattering his brothers' bare arms with fat red dots.

"I'm ogay. I'm ogay." To prove this, their dad chuckled and shrugged. "Dripped on my own feed."

"Pinch your nose, Dad. Hold your head back," said Raymond.

He did, and the flow of blood slowly stopped. When their dad began walking toward the door, he staggered again. Raymond and Rich caught him by either arm.

"I'm okay. I'm fine," he said, but he still allowed Ben's brothers to help him.

Ben held open the door. He looked down as his dad stumbled past, supported by his oldest sons. Ben dropped his helmet and shoulder pads on top of the shoes and followed at a distance.

He paused when they entered the kitchen. As expected, his mom went a little crazy.

"Oh my God. What happened?" Her voice was torn and nearly hysterical. "John, I told you, you need to use the cane. Look, look at your shirt! Your face!"

Ben quickly ducked into the long dining room and came out into the foyer, where he could creep upstairs and lock himself away in his bedroom.

He didn't want his brothers to see him cry.

When Ben awoke the next morning, the sun shone bright through the shutter slats, heating his room.

He lay on top of his covers. His sweat-drenched T-shirt lay on the floor, but his football pants were still on and still damp in the creases. He covered his face with a pillow, remembering the train of family members who had knocked on his door last night trying to get him to come out, at least to eat something. The final one was his dad, but that had started the waterworks all over again.

When sweat drizzled into his ear, he tossed the pillow, unlocked his bedroom door, and hit the shower. He dried off, put on a fresh T-shirt and a bathing suit, and crept downstairs. It was late morning, so the kitchen was quiet. Ben poured himself a bowl of Cheerios, a glass of orange juice, sat down, and took out his phone.

He texted Tuna, who was all in for a spin on their WaveRunners. Ben reminded him to bring a dry set of clothes and some sneakers for a snapping session later on. He was just putting his bowl in the sink when Rich and Jessica walked into the kitchen dressed in running gear. Sweat ran down their faces. Ben headed for the back door leading out on the deck.

Rich plucked a banana from the fruit bowl and broke it open. "Where you going, Bo?"

He couldn't not answer, but he opened the glass door before pausing. "WaveRunner. Meeting Tuna; then we're working on snaps."

"Hey, slow down. I'm talking to you." He spoke through a mouthful of banana.

"I gotta go, Rich. Tuna's probably waiting."

"Let him wait. I'm talking to you. This isn't last night." Rich took another bite.

"I'll let you two talk." Jessica knew, like Ben, that Rich's tone meant a lecture was coming. She quickly disappeared.

"Look, we're all upset about Dad, but we've got to make things as normal as possible. For him, yeah, but for Mom too. Get what I mean?" Rich pointed what was left of his banana at Ben. "You lock yourself away in your room, and a bad situation just gets worse. You understand why?"

Ben looked down at the floor but nodded that he got it. He almost told Rich about how he felt. That their dad slowly coming undone right before his eyes was too much to take. But that would only prolong a discussion that neither of them really wanted to have. So he looked up and met Rich's steady gaze, then nodded again until Rich said, "Okay, what time are you and Tuna planning to work on his snaps?"

"Uh, I don't know, two, maybe three? Why?"

"Well, I thought maybe I'd help out. He's never snapped before, right?" Rich said.

"Okay, two thirty, then."

"What, I don't get a thank you?" Rich popped the rest of the banana into his mouth.

"Thank you."

"Welcome," he said around his banana before swallowing. "So I'll have Thea come at three."

"What?" Ben looked to see if his brother was kidding.

He wasn't.

33

Ben shook his head and walked away, not waiting for Rich to explain why Thea had to ruin his afternoon. He grabbed a towel and headed out through his backyard and toward the water.

The lake was flat as a tabletop. Ben could see scattered rocks across the lakebed. They appeared to be within easy reach, but as Ben idled his machine out past the swim buoys, he knew the crystal clear water was seven feet deep and getting deeper fast. Once he was a safe distance from shore, he checked all around him, then took off at full throttle skimming across the flat water like a perfect skipping stone.

Tuna stood on the edge of his dock wearing a life jacket three sizes too small. His great white gut begged for some kind of covering, but as Ben coasted in, he could see that Tuna had slathered it with sunblock.

Ben stood up on his machine. "Hey, buddy. You ready?"

"Where we going?"

"I figured the rope swing. Then maybe back to town for a Johnny Angel's burger—"

"Or two," Tuna said.

"Or two." Ben grinned because even Raymond couldn't put down two Johnny Angel burgers. "Then we gotta get back to my house by two thirty cuz Rich is helping us with snaps."

Tuna made a face. "Rich? I thought we'd have some fun, you and me? Richie's a hard case. He'll probably make us do bear crawls."

Ben cut the engine of his machine. "We're not doing any bear crawls. He's gonna help make you our starting center."

Tuna snorted. "Like that's not gonna happen."

"Everyone knows you're our best lineman, Tuna, but you gotta be able to snap the ball too."

Tuna waved a hand. "If Ro could do it, I can do it."

"But that's what this is all about. Ro *couldn't* do it. It's not that easy. Did you see how happy he was to go back to guard?"

"Okay, okay. But no bear crawls."

"I promise." Ben raised his right hand.

Tuna gave one short nod and marched toward his WaveRunner.

They sped to the south end, where cliffs of shale rose a hundred feet up from the water. On a baby bluff, an old tree reached out over the water. They beached their machines and climbed to the top of the bluff. The rope hung limp from the twisted old tree. Ben hauled it up with a thin line, battered and gray, that was nailed to the tree.

"You wanna go?" Ben held out the thick knotted end to Tuna.

"Thanks." Tuna accepted the rope, backed up a few paces, ran, and launched himself into space.

With his feet on the knot and both hands gripping the thick rope, he swung his weight around so that he was facing Ben. At the height of the swing, Tuna launched himself free from the rope, did a backflip, and plunged into the aqua-green water below. It was a feat that belied Tuna's great bulk, and it explained why he was so good at playing football. Tuna was an athlete.

Ben hauled in the rope. No way was he doing a backflip, or any kind of stunt. If he got hurt, it would ruin the entire football season for his brothers and his dad. He clenched his hands around the rough hairy rope, backed up, and ran. A dizzying thrill took hold of him as the ground disappeared beneath his feet. Quickly, he clamped the knot between his feet so he could ride the rope to its highest point.

When he let go, Ben floated in the empty space. Time crawled like ketchup from the bottom of a bottle. Ben saw his father in a highlight reel slamming quarterbacks to the earth. Ben's father had been a captain of every team he'd ever played on, from Little League to the NFL, and he told Ben that if you wanted to lead you had to serve. He wondered why his father had been so keen for him to play the position of his foes rather than on the defensive line, like him. Then the words rang through his head.

"Every single play I would smash my head into some three-hundred-pound rhinoceros to sdop his charge. I did that,

112

whad? Ten thousand times? A hundred thousand? Ben, he's a quarderback. They barely get hit anymore."

Could he really expect to play football without getting hit?

"BEN!" Tuna screamed at the top of his lungs.

Ben suddenly realized that he was sideways and nearly upside down.

He hit the water with a terrible SMACK!

Then everything went dark.

Ben choked and sputtered.

He was facedown in the water. His life jacket had carried him to the surface. He kicked and flailed just as Tuna reached him. His friend flipped him over, grabbed a strap on the back of his jacket, and towed him back to shore with powerful leg kicks. Tuna rolled him on his side. Shale crackled beneath him. His legs hung out over the shelf, dangling in the water. He vomited water and what was left of his cereal, gagging and choking.

"Are you all right? What happened?" Tuna knelt beside him.

Ben struggled to his hands and knees, spitting bile onto the shale and shaking his head. "I . . . I don't know. I was . . . thinking, I guess."

"Thinking?" Tuna scrunched up his face.

"I don't know. Give me a hand, would you?" Ben got to his feet and tenderly massaged his neck. He winced.

"Oh boy. Oh boy, oh boy. Richie is gonna kill me."

"Why you? You practically saved my life." Ben looked at the dangling rope and the deep water beneath it.

"Because the messenger always gets shot."

"You're not the messenger."

"You know what I mean. Your brother is gonna blame me. He may not say it, but Tuna is gonna take the fall. Bear crawls forever." Tuna had real fear in his eyes.

"Don't worry, I'm fine." Ben swiveled his head around and gulped back the pain. "Let's go. I'll ice this baby up and he'll never know."

"I feel like he's a mind reader."

"He's a tough coach, but that's because he played for Coach O'Leary down at UCF. You should hear the stories; he's a madman."

"Well, Rich would make the old coach proud, that's for sure." Tuna picked an oval piece of the flat shale from beneath his feet. With a grunt he skipped it expertly across the water's surface. "Seventeen! Did you see that?"

"He's not that bad."

"Yeah? We'll see how 'not bad' he is if you keep touching your neck."

Ben and Tuna soaked in some more sun for the next hour, then got back on their WaveRunners and zipped across ten miles of water to Ben's house. They climbed the steps to Ben's kitchen beneath a canopy of river birch trees, their whispering leaves high overhead. They were hit by a frosty wall of air as they entered the house. Ben went straight to the fridge and filled a ziplock bag with handfuls of ice. They also grabbed some turkey wraps and cans of sweet iced tea.

Tuna scouted out the great room before they escaped downstairs to the theater room, where five Xboxes waited for them. Ben sat back in a reclining chair and packed the ice around the back of his neck. They played a few games of *Fortnite* with Malik and Woody, who were both online, while they ate their wraps.

Before they knew it, Ben's ice was nearly all melted and his phone said 2:00.

"We gotta go."

"I got a gold rocket launcher. Let's finish this game." Tuna's eyes were locked on the screen.

Ben got up and powered down Tuna's Xbox. "You'll thank me later. Rich always says that if you're early you're on time, if you're on time you're late, and if you're late you're done."

Tuna mumbled about his gold rocket launcher, but he was only two steps behind Ben, up the stairs and into the mudroom, where they put on sneakers, then jogged up the driveway to the grass sports field where Rich was looking at his watch.

He looked up. "You're late."

"We're five minutes early." Ben gave Tuna an I-told-you-so look.

"You need to be fifteen minutes early to be on time. What's wrong with your neck?"

"What? Nothing. Why?"

"Your head looks funny." Rich poked Ben's neck. "You been icing it? What happened? You crash the WaveRunner?"

"No." Ben's stomach clenched. "I slept on it wrong."

"You two goofballs better be careful on those stupid WaveRunners. That's all we need." Rich shot a glare at the both of them.

"Can we work on snaps?" Ben tried to sound respectful even though he didn't feel that way.

"Well, I thought since you guys are late, we'll warm up with some bear crawls."

Tuna's eyes widened and his jaw dropped.

"Rich, come on," Ben pleaded.

Rich scowled at him. "Come on, what? You guys show up late, you crawl."

Tuna gave Ben a nasty look.

Ben turned to his brother ready to beg, but Rich broke out in a wide grin and punched Ben lightly on the shoulder. "Gotcha."

"Not funny, Rich."

Tuna chuckled with relief.

"Tuna, I want you to watch me." Rich picked up a ball from the grass and held it over his head with both hands. "You're right-handed like me, so you want to have the fingers of your right hand on the laces. See?"

Tuna nodded.

"Okay, so a shotgun snap is really just a short pass between your legs. So we're gonna begin by just getting our hands right and we're gonna use our left hand to guide the ball where we want it to go. Okay? Let's try it." Rich backed up only about five yards from Tuna and zipped the ball directly at the big boy's chest.

Tuna caught it, smiled, and threw it back at Rich. The wobbling duck was to the left of Rich's knees, but he snatched it up and reloaded. "That's okay. Focus on the spin, not where it goes. We can fix that."

Back and forth they went, with Rich coaching patiently and Tuna scowling harder and harder. Finally, Tuna let one fly that wasn't a duck. It wasn't a spiral either, but almost.

"See? That'll work!" Rich's excitement put a smile on Tuna's face.

Now the pace picked up, until at last Rich said, "Okay,

good. Ben, you ready?"

Ben lined up about four yards behind Tuna and clapped his hands. "Oh yeah."

"Okay, Tuna, you know the cadence. On the first go unless it's play number eight. Ice. If it's play number eight, what do you do?"

"Ice" was what the linemen said to each other on play eight to remind themselves to freeze and not give in to the itch.

"That's the freeze play, so I freeze. I don't move," said Tuna.

Rich nodded. "That's right. Now, it's a hard count and you'll be just itching to snap the ball, but if you can't stop yourself from scratching that itch, then you can't play center. Got it?"

"Got it, Coach."

"Okay, set the ball down and place your hands the same way you just did over your head. Don't put too much weight forward. You need to be able to snap it without falling on your face. That's it. Good. Now you're aiming for the center of Ben's chest, right where his number will be." Rich patted Ben's chest. "Ben, I'll call the play number because I don't have the cards, and I'll run the route of the primary receiver so you can get some work too. Let's get five snaps to warm up; then we'll run plays. Go."

Ben called out his cadence, and Tuna snapped a worm burner.

"That's all right," said Rich. "You're getting warmed up. Just like you did over your head. Go."

This time it was over Ben's head. Ben jumped for it, and a bolt of pain exploded in his neck. He clenched his teeth, biting back the pain, angry with Tuna.

"You're zeroing in," Rich said. "Again. Go."

Tuna had one that wasn't bad, then a bad one before another decent one. When they began to run plays, Tuna fell apart. His snaps were all over the place, with just one hitting Ben in the center of his chest. When Rich called play eight, Tuna snapped it anyway, an irretrievable duck off to Ben's left. In a real game that would be a disaster. When they finished, Tuna hung his head.

"Hey, none of that, big guy." Rich shook Tuna's shoulder. "You're just starting out. It takes hundreds of snaps to get good at it. You're an athlete. You'll get there with practice. Get your dad out in the yard and just snap, snap, snap."

"Okay, Coach." Tuna raised his head, then let it fall again.

At that moment, a pickup truck rolled through the gates. All three of them looked over.

Rich looked at his watch. "Right on time. Stick around, big guy. Maybe Thea will give you some incentive to get out in your yard."

"Hey," Ben said. "It's three o'clock. We were five minutes early and you called us late."

"You never heard of chivalry?"

"Like Knights of the Round Table?" Ben rubbed his neck as Thea jumped out of the truck, a newer blue one driven by her mother.

"Exactly. The code of honor," Rich said, returning the mother's wave. "Chivalry is not dead."

"That's hogwash," Ben muttered as Thea sprinted toward them with her helmet on and buckled up tight.

"No, that's just having manners, little brother." Rich had a good laugh at his and Tuna's expense. "Hello, Thea. You ready? You look ready."

"Yes, sir, I am. And I'm sorry we're late. My mom's truck broke down a mile down the road, and we had to walk back and get my brother's truck. He was working in the fields with the keys in his pocket or we'd have been here at two thirty. You know Vince Lombardi said if you're not a half hour early, you're late."

Ben put a hand over his face, and Tuna snickered.

"I didn't know he said that, but I like it." Rich cast an evil look at Ben. "Okay, let's get going. Thea, I want you to get that ball and hold it with two hands over your head like this."

Thea stared intently at Ben's brother through her face mask. "Uh, Coach. I don't mean to be rude in any way, but I can already snap. I don't want you to waste your time on the basics. I mean, I'll do it if you want, but I'm good if you don't mind."

Rich had another laugh. "Well, let's see what you got."

Ben gave Tuna a secret look, sneering and snorting quietly while shaking his head. He lined up five yards away to make it even more difficult for her, and he extended his hands.

"Now, the cadence is—"

"I know, Coach, color, number, color, number, down, set, go. Unless it's ice. Then it's a hard count and I don't snap the ball." Thea said it like it was no big deal.

Rich stared at her. "How . . . how did you know?"

She shrugged. "You ran the hard count last night with Sol. The D line all jumped."

"Oh. That's good. Good on you to pick that up." Rich was obviously impressed.

Thea shrugged again. "Yeah, my brothers have all these calls they make. I just keep my mouth shut and listen. You can figure out a lot if you listen."

"Okay, well, let's see you snap." Rich nodded to Ben.

Ben didn't know what to make of this girl. He glanced at Tuna, who made a doubting face, like he thought she was a sham.

"Go, Ben," Rich said.

Ben extended his hands again. "Blue ten, blue ten, Down. Set! Go!"

The football came out from between Thea's feet in a blur.

Ben closed his hands to catch it, but the point of the perfect spiral had already bounced off his chest. "Umph!"

Ben staggered back a couple steps. The ball rolled all five yards back to Thea.

She scooped it up. "Another?"

Ben checked himself from shouting at her to take it easy, but he could never say that, never admit that a girl snapped it too hard for him to handle. What would Rich say to that?

Ben made a big show of rubbing his right eye. He'd almost been blinded in an accident when he was just seven, and he wore a contact lens in that eye. "Yeah, my contact. Something got in it."

"Hey, are you okay?" Rich showed real concern. He put an arm around Ben's shoulders and bent over to examine the eye. The whole family was sensitive about his eye, and Ben played it.

"I think I got it." Ben gently pushed Rich away. "I'm good. Let's go."

"Okay. Hey, Thea, excellent snap. Outstanding." Rich returned to his spot in the grass.

Ben stayed five yards away, this time for his own benefit. Thea looked at him as if she knew he was faking with his contact lens, and he felt his face get extra hot. She seemed to be satisfied with his discomfort because she smiled and winked at him before getting into her stance with both hands placed perfectly on the ball.

He called out the cadence, and she snapped another bullet at his chest. Ben had brothers too, and he'd caught plenty of passes in the lawn from Rich, a D1 quarterback. He knew how to handle heat, and he caught the snap without having the wind knocked out of him. Still, it stung his hands like a swarm of bees.

"Excellent!" Rich laughed with delight.

Ben was dumbfounded, and judging by the look on his face, so was Tuna. He just couldn't imagine going through the entire season having a girl, and a skinny girl at that, playing center on an O line that otherwise was stacked with beef.

"Who taught you to snap?" Rich asked.

Thea shrugged. "When my brothers had friends, the only position they'd let me play was all-time center. And they wouldn't even let me play that, unless I could put it right in the quarterback's hands. They showed me how, and they put a bull's-eye on the side of the barn so I could practice."

Rich looked at her with delight. "This is really great. You're our starting center. That's it. Tuna, you're back protecting Ben's blind side, but I still want you practicing snaps in case Thea gets injured. I'll give you some reps there in practice, so don't let me down. You can't play a spread offense unless you can get the ball to the quarterback on the snap. Let's run some plays."

Tuna and Ben traded glances as they got in position. They ran a couple dozen plays, and Thea never wavered. Every single snap was on the mark, and a bullet. The blue pickup rumbled back through the gates at three-thirty. Ben was relieved. His hands hurt worse than his neck.

"Thanks, Coach! Bye!" Thea waved, then turned and ran toward the truck, her braids bouncing. It was somehow insulting.

They ditched Rich and made their way back to Ben's house. They huddled up down on the dock.

"We got to admit it. She's good." Ben looked Tuna in the eye trying to get a read on his thoughts.

"I can do that. I just gotta practice. Richie even said so. What? We gonna have some string-bean girl on our O line?" Tuna snorted like a bull as he pulled on his life jacket. "I don't think so. Put the Big Tuna at center, now Rohan's got your blind side, and he's a mauler. So Omar plays left guard, Big Jake at right, and you know they're gonna have Luke Logan go both ways, so he's our right tackle, and we are jacked!"

Ben was still doubtful, but he smiled. "Positive thinking. That's good."

Tuna untied his machine and mounted up. "You better positive think some more ice on that neck. I told you Richie is a mind reader. He jumped right on it. Scary, dude, scary."

"Shoulda seen your face when he said bear crawls."

Tuna fired up his machine. "Yeah, well I'm waitin' to see that girl's face when Woody gets her tonight."

"What's he gonna do?" Ben tried not to look or sound worried, even though he was.

Tuna shrugged. "I don't know. But you know if it's Woody it's gonna be a good prank. Maybe she even quits? Then?

"Problem solved."

37

Ben had an early dinner with his family. Outside, tall purple-bellied clouds over the lake promised stormy trouble. Ben's dad checked the weather app on his phone between almost every bite of his roasted chicken and mashed potatoes with gravy. Ben's neck was killing him despite taking two Advils. He was praying for not just rain. They would still practice in that. What he needed was some lightning, even thunder would do.

His dad gulped down a loaded forkful of food and looked at Raymond. "I think this'll pass over and we should have a window for practice. There'll be another band moving through around eight. Do you want to do team defense after agilities to be safe?"

While Ben and his brothers had gotten used to the way their dad's speech was a little garbled, and it started to sound like regular speech to them, Ben could tell by the way Raymond listened intently that even he was having trouble understanding this time. It seemed that their dad's speech had gotten a little bit worse.

"Naw, Rich can have it." Raymond wore a devilish smile. "He needs it. They can't even get the snap off."

Their dad took a swig of milk, then looked at Rich. "How did Tuna look?"

"You mean how did *Thea* look? Amazing. She's our starting center, no ifs, ands, or buts. Every snap, bam! Right into Ben's chest, like bullets." Rich winked at Ben. "Tuna needs a lot of work. I'm hoping he gets better so he can be our backup."

Outside on the darkened lake, distant thunder rumbled.

Their dad shook his head slowly, and he chuckled under his breath. "And the Auburn guys wanted to make her a cheerleader."

"I need to get her at least *some* reps on defense," said Raymond. "She's got to start at free safety."

Ben sat quiet while the whole table discussed Thea and her twin brothers and then the wider subject of girls and football.

Rich's girlfriend, Jessica, said, "Didn't Coach Sindoni ask Rose to play running back?"

"And she could have too. She had the speed and the toughness." Their dad looked at Rose with obvious pride.

Rose looked at her plate, blushing. She was lean and muscular, not some skinny chicken like Thea.

Ben wondered if he should text Woody and tell him whatever prank he had planned to forget it.

"Weren't you the one who said she couldn't play?" Cara was a structural engineer who believed girls could do anything.

"Only because I didn't want her to get hurt. Lacrosse was her ticket. My ticket was football, so I didn't ski, even though I wanted to," said their dad. Ben leaned in to concentrate on understanding what his dad was saying. "If she didn't have offers to go wherever she wanted for lacrosse, I would have loved for her to play football."

Ben secretly took the phone out of his pocket, even though they weren't allowed to have phones at the table. He had it on his lap and began to type out a message to Woody. He glanced down just to check if he was getting it right.

Lightning struck close to the house, and the crack of thunder rattled the windows. When he looked up, his dad was glaring at him, and he held out a trembling hand. "You know the rules. You think I'm so sick there's no more rules? Give it here. I want to see what's so important that you break the no-phone rule."

38

Ben hesitated just a moment, just long enough to switch apps blindly under the table. He passed the phone to his dad.

"*Clash of Clans*? Really, Ben? You just lost your phone for the rest of the day, buddy. Next time it'll be a week." His dad struggled to get the phone into his pocket but finally got it.

His dad wasn't finished. "You know, another reason I didn't want Rose to play was her having to deal with a bunch of meatheads. Guys can sometimes—a lot of times—be upset if a girl can outdo them in something. You know what I mean?"

Ben nodded. Everyone was looking at him.

"If Thea can snap," said his dad, "then we're lucky to have her. *You're* lucky. And I want you to act that way. You're a leader, and the other guys will follow what you do. Got it?"

"Got it, Dad."

"Good."

The thunderstorm raged outside, and the conversation turned to Rose's summer internship at the district attorney's office. Ben zoned out. He took his dad's words seriously. Even though he couldn't stand Thea, he had to admit that she would help the team, and him personally, if she could get the ball into his hands every time. He wondered how he could get her to take some heat off the ball. He certainly couldn't ask her. Maybe Rich could?

After fifteen minutes, the worst of the storm had finally passed.

Dinner ended with everyone telling their mom how good it was and everyone helping to clean up. Ben's dad struggled to get up from the table, and without saying anything Rich grabbed his arm and helped him to his feet. Ben got the okay from his mom to go get his equipment on.

On the drive to the field, Ben began to worry about Woody again. He never should have encouraged his friend, but Thea was so arrogant and sharp-tongued. Her attitude was somehow worse because she was pretty on top of everything else. Outside, the dark clouds had been replaced by blue skies and sunshine glittering in the rain-drenched grass and trees.

They got to the field fifteen minutes early. Woody was nowhere to be seen. Thea was there already, snapping to Sol. For some unknown reason, this made Ben angry.

Tuna pulled up in his sister's Volvo with his helmet already on.

"Let's go." Rich grabbed Ben by the shoulder pad, then cupped his hands around his mouth. "Tuna, with us! Let's go!"

Rich took off on a jog for the far end zone, probably to

spare Tuna any embarrassment for his wayward snaps.

Rich looked at his watch. "Okay, we got ten solid minutes. Let's work on this."

Tuna was wildly inconsistent, but Rich never wavered in his encouragement, nor did Ben. Maybe it wasn't too late. Maybe Tuna could rebound and Thea would be too light to be an effective blocker. In his excitement, Ben forgot about Woody until Raymond blew his whistle. Woody wasn't in Ben's agility group, and when that ended, Rich grabbed him right away to work on his passing while everyone else did Oklahomas.

When the next whistle sounded, it signaled a water break. Ben knew he could finally talk to Woody. Even though he didn't want Thea snapping the ball to him, he didn't want to have anything bad happen to her. He thought of his sister Rose.

"Whoa, where you goin', champ?"

"Water."

Rich's mouth fell open. "Water? You're not even sweating. Oh, all right. Just give me one more hitch and go."

Ben threw the pass and took off for where his teammates were gathered on the far sideline, helmets off, drinking their water. As he ran, he couldn't help but notice the dark sky had returned beyond the treetops to the south. Distracted by the tall brooding thunderclouds, Ben didn't see what caused the bloodcurdling scream that sounded out across the field.

He was ten yards from his water bottle, but he pulled up short.

Thea was on her knees in the wet grass, sobbing.

Woody had something hanging from his clenched hand.

He held it up for everyone to see, turning in a slow circle while everyone laughed. In his other hand he held a pair of pruning shears, a kind of scissors used to cut small branches and stems. As Ben approached Woody, his stomach did a flip. The thing he held was half of one of Thea's blonde braids.

"Woody, what the—" Ben couldn't help himself. He charged his friend and blasted him with open hands, knocking him on his butt. In the shocked silence, the only thing they heard was Thea's soft sobbing.

"What?" Disbelief filled Woody's eyes as he stared up at Ben. "You were in on it."

"I texted you," Ben growled.

"You texted me 'Woody I don't think.' What's that supposed to mean?"

Raymond was the first coach to arrive, and he knelt beside Thea with an arm around her shoulder and his forehead nearly touching hers. Thea's mom wasn't far behind. She hugged her daughter to her chest and cast a look so savage around the team that no one could meet her eyes.

"I texted you, Woody! I texted, 'I don't think you should do anything to Thea.'"

Woody remained on the ground. "That's a lie!"

Out of nowhere, Rich appeared, his face twisted with disgust. "Ben, you were in on this? Woody, what were you thinking?"

Suddenly, Woody's face puckered up, turned red, and he began to cry. "All the guys knew! They wanted me to do it!"

Rich scowled at Ben, but it was child's play compared to the look on his dad's face as he came up on the scene after struggling to walk across the field with his cane.

"What happened?" Thea's mom looked at Ben's dad with confusion. Ben remembered that other people couldn't understand his dad as clearly as he could.

Raymond understood, though. "Dad, Woody cut off her braid."

"Everyone knew!" Woody wailed like someone had cut off his leg, and he tossed the evidence aside.

"Ben knew about it, Dad." Rich pinched his lips together.

"And . . . and everyone!" Woody had reduced his volume to a whine.

Ben could see by looking around that he wasn't the only one who wanted to strangle his friend.

Ben's dad looked at Thea's mom. "Is she gonna be okay?"

Thea's mom squinted for a moment. Ben knew she was trying hard to understand his dad's speech. She then gave a short nod. "She'll be fine. She grew up with two older brothers, so she's a tough one, though I've got to say, they never did anything as rattlesnake mean as this. Now we'll have to cut it all back, and this girl did like her hair down in church."

Ben's dad nodded. "Well, I'm very sorry, Mrs. Labourdette. Thea's a really good player. I will fix this, I promise. Nothing like this will ever happen again. I'm sorry that it happened at all, I really am."

Ben's dad knelt down beside Thea and would have tipped over if Raymond hadn't caught him. "Hey, you gonna be okay?"

Thea sniffed and nodded.

Ben's dad rubbed her back. "Hey, Thea. No one on this team is gonna be anything but nice to you from now on. I promise. And you're so pretty you could have no hair at all. You know that?" Thea sniffed and nodded and quietly laughed.

"That's good." Ben's dad gently patted her back and gave Raymond a look to help him up.

Once Ben's dad was on his feet, he said, "Come on, guys, bring it in close."

Ben was surprised by his dad's tone. Instead of growling and barking like the mad dog he'd expected, Ben's dad sounded sad and tired.

"Okay, we're a team, right?" Ben's dad looked around at all their faces. "Yeah. We are. And that means we're all for each other. We can't care if someone's different from us. We're a team. If you're the best player or the worst, you're still on the team, and you're just as valuable. That's a team."

His dad paused to look around again. Ben noticed a lot of his teammates looking down, and he knew they were only understanding some of what his dad was saying. Ben tried to catch his brother's eye, to make him take over for his dad, but it didn't happen and his dad continued. "Some people are different. Thea's a girl. Malik's got dark skin. Omar has a different religion. Look at me. I talk different. Maybe you have a hard time understanding what I say. I limp and I have a cane because of some old football injuries.

"Heck, you're going to go places in your life and people are gonna be different and you can't be afraid or mean. You gotta be kind. That's called tolerance."

Ben couldn't help noticing the dark sky creeping up behind his dad.

Suddenly his dad's voice hardened. "Boys, I gotta tell you, I think we can win every game this season, including Penn Yan. Win a championship. But I don't give a hoot about winning if you aren't going to respect and be kind to other people, especially your teammates. Now, Woody, what you did is wrong, but you're not alone. A lot of guys knew what you were going to do, and that makes them just as wrong as you. Isn't that right, Benjamin?"

Ben withered beneath his father's stare. He couldn't speak.

Thankfully, his dad went on.

"For those of you who didn't know, I'm sorry, but this whole team needs to remember this, remember my words. Now get your helmets on and line up on this sideline. Raymond, they'll run cross-fields that way and bear crawls back until I blow my whistle. Not you, Thea." Ben's dad turned and headed for his chair with Rich alongside, grabbing his arm in case he stumbled.

They ran, and they crawled, ran and crawled, ran and crawled. Raymond's whistle was a torment to the body and mind. The dark sky slithered over their heads and opened up. The pouring rain was so thick it made it even harder to breathe. The bigger guys began to vomit and drop, misty gray hulks in the flooded grass. Still the sharp bark of Raymond's whistle tormented them.

The pain in Ben's neck made him dizzy.

Finally, God put an end to it with a rumble of thunder.

Ben's dad blew his whistle immediately. He pointed to the parking lot where all the parents had retreated to their cars long ago. The team staggered like zombies through a graveyard until they were snapped up by the waiting cars and trucks.

Rich helped their dad into the passenger seat of the big black Ford Expedition. Ben climbed in back with Rich. Raymond drove in silence. Rainwater trickled down their faces and arms, pooling on the leather seats. The windows steamed over.

As they turned onto 41A, Rich cleared his throat. "I just hope we didn't lose half the team."

Their dad didn't move a muscle. "We won."

"I don't know, Dad. They're eleven- and twelve-year-old kids."

Now their dad turned. "Richard, they'll never forget this, and they'll never forget what it was about. A little rain, a little throw-up. That's football."

Rich drew up a play of Xs and Os on his steamed over window. "This isn't the NFL, Dad."

"I know what it is. I saw the hairy eyeballs the parents were giving me. They already asked their kids what it was about, I promise you. And I'm not gonna let kids on any team I coach mistreat another kid. I'm just not." Their dad turned back to face the front.

A smattering of parents had remained outside their cars, under umbrellas. Ben had seen the looks on their faces, and he feared that Rich was right.

He just hoped the season wouldn't be over before it had started.

It thundered all night.

Several times the crash and jolt of brilliant white light in his bedroom window awakened Ben with a start. He'd remain awake until the low, distant rumbling lulled him back to sleep, only to be awakened again later on by a brand-new storm.

Finally, when he woke and the gray light of morning coaxed him out of bed, he peered out the window and saw low clouds drizzling rain and mist across the lake. Thankfully, his neck felt much better, or maybe it was just because the rest of his body ached from the endless sprints and bear crawls. He hobbled downstairs.

"Hi, honey." Ben's mom was in the kitchen. "I'll make you an omelet. You want ham in it?"

"Yes, please." He sat down at the table while his mom filled the kitchen with wonderful smells. He worried all the while whether or not they'd have enough people to field a team.

His mom set breakfast before him, then sat down herself with a cup of coffee.

"Where's Dad?"

"He had meetings all day at the firm." His mom lowered her head to make eye contact with him. "How's your legs?"

"Tired. Sore." Ben cut into the omelet with the side of his fork. Steam floated up into his nose.

His mom reached over and gave his left hand a squeeze. "You know, your dad is going through a lot."

"I know, Mom, but people were puking their guts out in the pouring rain. This isn't the NFL. I don't know if we'll even have a team after what Dad made us do."

"You should eat." His mom pointed to his plate with her mug of coffee. "That was mean, what Woody did. If someone did that to Rose, I'd be crazy."

"I guess."

"And your father said you knew he was going to do it." She scowled at him.

"He said he was gonna do something, Mom. I didn't know what, and I tried to text him not to at dinner and Dad took my phone."

"Eat, it's getting cold." She pointed with her mug again before taking a swig.

"Okay." He shoveled the bite of omelet into his mouth.

His mom got up. She placed her hand on top of his head and mussed up his hair. "You be nice to that girl, Benjamin. You know better."

He swallowed. "I know. I will."

He watched her go, finished breakfast, and went downstairs.

The Xbox was the gathering place for rainy days. Ben put his headset on and logged in to his account. Half his team was on. He joined a party with Tuna, Rohan, Malik, and Luke Logan to play a game of *Siege*.

For a while, they just played, but between battles, the uncomfortable silence began to make Ben's skin crawl.

Finally, Ben had to break the ice. "Is anybody as sore as me?"

Everyone began talking at once.

"Legs are killing me."

"Torture."

"How about Woody?"

"My groin."

"Vomit burned my throat."

"Your dad lost it."

"I thought we'd be there all night."

"That thunder saved my life."

Then silence.

Ben broke it. "Everyone's coming to practice tonight, though, right?"

More silence, and Ben's heart ached.

Finally, Malik said, "Even if I wanted to, and I don't, my dad would never let me quit."

Rohan said, "My mom is as crazy as Ben's dad. She'd *never* let me quit. She and my dad were both mad at me, and I didn't even do anything."

Luke and Tuna agreed that parents were generally crazy.

"Your dad was right about what he said, though," Malik

said. "About people treating you different."

"Who treats you different?" Tuna sounded offended.

Malik laughed bitterly. "Man, I go into a store in town? The shopkeepers follow me around like I'm gonna *steal* something. Me and my family go into Johnny's, sit down, and people get up and move to another table like they're gonna catch the flu or something? My mom and dad are *doctors*. What is *that*?"

"Oh, I'm sorry, bro," Tuna said quietly.

More silence.

"So maybe we should treat her like she's one of us. . . ."

"She *is* one of us."

"She can sure snap the ball," Ben said.

"She can hit too."

"Let's win a championship."

"Beat Penn Yan."

"Yeah, we're gonna kick their butts!"

The rain let up to a drizzle.

It didn't matter to Ben's dad. "This isn't baseball," he said.

On the drive to practice, the sun began to poke through the clouds. The hot, steamy field squished under Ben's feet. Thea still had her braids, but they were baby braids now.

Ben went to her directly. "Hey."

She had a football and tossed it spinning into the air. "Hey yourself."

Ben jumped and snapped up the ball. "Look, I'm sorry about what happened. I tried to stop it. I really did, but I gotta tell you, you're not helping yourself with that attitude."

She glared at him, and he was surprised by the genuine hatred. "I'm—I'm trying to help you."

"Yeah? I saw your face when I said I could snap. You did everything you could to have your cow patty of a friend be there 'cause you didn't want to take snaps from a girl. And you want to play quarterback? Quarterback is for leaders. You think Patrick Mahomes would care who snapped him the ball if it could help them win?"

Thea's words cut Ben to the bone. His blood boiled in an instant. He was so mad that the wicked reply got gummed up in his throat. He sputtered and stuttered and realized that the reason why he was so angry was that she was right!

"No. He wouldn't care. And I don't either. I didn't just come to apologize. I came to get some work with you, and also ask you a favor." He spun the ball back in the air so it landed in her hands.

She looked at him with obvious suspicion. "What favor?"

Ben managed to smile. "Can you take some heat off the ball? I'd like to keep some skin on my hands."

Thea grinned. "I won't tell you that my brothers don't complain."

Ben returned her smile. "Good. And I mean this in a good way. I hear your brothers are animals."

"And now I won't have to turn them loose on you." She put the ball down on the goal line. "Let's work. You get lined up on the five, or the four if you want."

"Wait. What? Your brothers? Really?" He lined up on the four.

"Kidding."

"Oh."

They got to work, and Ben's appreciation for Thea grew with each snap. Now that she wasn't trying to punish him, her snaps were crisp, accurate, and smooth as silk.

"I mean, if you can do this in a game?" Ben snorted with amusement. "It's gonna make the play at least another second faster, and I'll be able to keep my eyes on the defense instead of watching for a snap that could be over my head or down in the grass."

It was nearly time for warm-ups when they called it and jogged toward the group of teammates clustered in the opposite end zone. Amid the milling bunch, a pale white globe shone like a beacon.

"I don't believe it." Ben stopped in his tracks at the sight.

"Believe what?" Thea stopped too. "Oh. Gosh."

Ben and Thea walked the rest of the way toward their teammates in the end zone. Woody saw them and met them on the field.

He was bald as a baby.

Gone was the wild mop of curly brown hair that the girls went crazy for. His scalp was as pale as a waterlogged worm.

"What do you say? What do you know?" Also gone was Woody's usual wise-guy energy. His head hung low. "I know it's not the same, but my parents figured I should chop my own hair to kind of, you know, be with you. I'm really sorry for what I did."

Woody peeked up to see what she would say.

"That's okay, Woody. Let's just win some football games." Thea held out her hand, and Woody shook it.

When they got to the team part of practice, where the offense and defense went live like a mini scrimmage, Ben and his offense gave Raymond fits. Not only did Thea's perfect snaps help the plays hit faster, her absence on defense created a hole that no one else seemed able to fill. When Tuna substituted in for her, his snaps were wild, the offense stalled, and Thea was knocking kids down all over the field. Her acceptance by the team seemed to supercharge her performance.

After practice, Ben's dad had Rich gather everyone around him. "Guys, and girl, that was a championship practice. And good for you to learn a lesson. Woody, you're still pretty, even without your hair, and I appreciate what you did. That's called solidarity. . . . Raymond, say it for me so they understand."

"Solidarity," said Raymond.

"Thank you. We're all in this together. We're a team. Now, I want you to go home tonight and thank your parents for letting you play football. It's a lot of back-and-forth for them and a lot of dirty uniforms to wash, so you thank them, okay?"

"Yes, Coach!"

"Okay. We're three days in and we already look like champions. We got a week and a half before we scrimmage Geneva, then it's game week and we open with Jordan Elbridge. Woody, you break 'em down."

Woody beamed with joy, and he stood in the center of the team. They all began to clap in unison, chanting, "Huh! Huh! Huh! Huh!" They copied Woody's increasing intensity and pace until he shouted, "Break it down!"

Then, in unison again, everyone screamed at the top of their lungs.

"Ahhhh!"

Sunday was the first day off from practice.

Ben had Tuna and a few other teammates over for a sleepover. They played Xbox until midnight and horsed around until all hours before finally falling asleep. So when Ben felt someone tugging on his big toe, he said, "Tuna, no. Stop."

The tugging only got harder.

Ben threw the sleeping bag off his head, kicked his feet, and cried, "Enough, man!"

A hand grabbed his ankle, a big hand with a weak grip. His dad pushed a finger to his own lips. "Shh. Church."

"Aww, Dad."

"It's the last time for a while. We've got games until November." His dad gave him a sad look, shrugged, and walked out.

Ben pulled the covers back over his head and closed his eyes. He was determined to go back to sleep, but it wasn't five minutes before he swept away his covers and reluctantly crawled out of the sleeping bag.

Upstairs, he found his dad at the kitchen table with a steaming mug of coffee. "Hey, you're up."

The joy on his dad's face rewarded him more than he felt he deserved. It wasn't a big deal, going to church. He didn't totally get the whole thing, but his dad took a strange delight in having Ben with him. He'd lean down to whisper in Ben's ear from time to time, mostly explaining things that Ben had heard before. Afterward, his dad would take him to the bakery for whatever he wanted.

He knew the church duty had fallen on his brothers and sisters as they were growing up. They had a four-man rotation growing up, sometimes five when their mom would break down and go with him, even though she was Jewish. He figured that's why his dad didn't force him to go, since there was no longer any rotation to speak of.

"Yeah," Ben said. "We turned in at midnight, but then we talked for a while."

His dad smiled. "Uh-huh."

"Can I wear my sneakers?"

"Your new ones. And pants!" His dad raised his voice because Ben was already around the corner. "And a collared shirt!"

Outside on the church steps, they were greeted by the reverend. "Good morning, Ben. Good morning, John. I hear your team is looking good."

"Hi, Craig. We are. Hopefully an undefeated season this year."

The reverend wore a look of genuine concern, no doubt because of his dad's slurred speech. "John, I, umm, noticed the cane. Is everything all right?"

Ben knew his dad was good friends with the reverend, that his dad had coached the reverend's son when he'd coached the high school wrestling team for Raymond. So Ben expected a full confession from his dad.

"Just another old football injury."

Ben looked up at his dad's face. He wore no sign of shame. Ben wanted to ask how his father could lie to the reverend like that, but he didn't dare.

They sat in the back corner, as always. His dad took the bulletin handed to them at the door and began to read. He wouldn't raise his head unless someone stopped and greeted him, some he obviously knew and some he didn't.

Ben was used to that. Although his dad was more than twenty years removed from his pro career and thirty from college, some people still described him as a hometown hero. He had grown up in Syracuse and stayed home to play college football at Syracuse University rather than accept a full ride to powerhouses like Penn State, Ohio State, Alabama, or Notre Dame.

The organ geared up, and Reverend Lindsey marched down the aisle with a large Bible and followed by a girl Ben recognized from his grade. She carried a long brass rod with a flame at its end to light the candle atop the altar. The organ kicked up a refrain, and everyone stood to sing. His dad opened a hymnal, held it between them, and pointed to the words as he croaked out the hymn. Ben never sang, but still his father pointed.

His dad's voice had never been very good, but now he struggled to sing every word. Ben watched with concern while his dad had trouble just to breathe. The hymn ended. They sat. Ben could see his dad was upset. His dad caught Ben looking, forced a smile, and gripped Ben's knee with one of his enormous hands.

The service droned on. Ben tried to pay attention, but his mind was on his dad. The sermon was something about trees and fruit, some good and some bad to be cut down and thrown into a fire. What Ben wanted to know was how God could allow things like ALS to even exist? And if it did, shouldn't it happen to bad people? His dad was good, a good tree with good fruit. He did all kinds of charity work, talked about how important it was to be nice to people, especially if they were different, went to church. It didn't make sense.

They stood. Reverend Lindsey told them to go forth and do good things. The organ kicked up again, and they walked out into the sunshine and the swaying trees casting their leafy shadows onto the sidewalk.

They headed over to the bakery, which teemed with churchgoers from other churches. His dad ordered a cappuccino and a box of doughnuts for the house. Ben got a turkey club sandwich, raspberry soda, and a smiley-face cookie. They found an empty table and sat.

Ben took a bite of his sandwich, then a swig of soda before he spoke. "Dad?"

"Hmm?"

"Why didn't you tell Reverend Lindsey what's going on?" Ben took another pull on his soda to appear casual. People had to notice his father's speech. It seemed to be worsening by the day.

His dad turned his cup on the table, thinking, then sighing before he looked Ben in the eye. "I don't want people to feel sorry for me. Everyone understands old football injuries. You say you've got ALS, and they think you'll be dead by Christmas."

Ben nodded like he understood even though he didn't. "But the reverend, I figured . . ."

"Yeah, well . . ." He paused. "Thanks for coming with me today. It'll be the last time, like I said, until November. Eat, Bo."

He ate, but between every bite, he nearly choked on the question he wanted to ask, but somehow couldn't.

Ben's stomach was in knots. He breathed with short rapid breaths and his hands trembled.

They left the bakery in silence, but when they got into his dad's black Mercedes G 55, Ben buckled his seat belt and blurted it out.

"So will you?"

"Will I what, Bo?"

"Make it till Christmas, Dad."

45

His father's pause lasted a lifetime.

There they sat in their parking spot on a quietly busy street. Tourists in shorts and flip-flops mixed with churchgoers in Sunday finery gave the sidewalks a festive atmosphere. All the while Ben's insides froze over.

Finally Ben's dad looked up from the steering wheel. "I could get hit by a bus tomorrow. No one knows when their time is up, Bo."

He looked away from his dad. A little girl walking with her mom had a powdered doughnut. White sugar covered the front of her red dress.

His dad put a hand on his shoulder. "Hey. People can live with this for a long time, and I believe they'll find a cure in the next ten years, so all I have to do is hang on. That's my plan."

Ben covered the giant hand with his own. "That sounds good."

His dad smiled and gave Ben's shoulder a feeble squeeze before he fired up the engine.

At home they found the whole family but Raymond and Cara at the kitchen table with their mom making pancakes and bacon. Ben's friends had all been picked up by their parents. He put the box of doughnuts on the big lazy Susan in the center of the table and sat between his dad and Jessica. They ate and talked and laughed and agreed to meet down at the water for a boat ride later.

"I need to get some weightlifting in first," their dad said. The doctor had told his dad that lifting weights would help keep his muscles toned. "Rich?"

"Sorry, Dad. Raymond and I lifted already."

"Bo?"

"Sure." His dad would only let him lift very light weights for high reps. He looked forward to the day he could load up the bars with Raymond and Rich and hear the sweet crash of metal from his own lifting rather than the dinky clink of five- and ten-pound dumbbells returning to their racks.

The weight room was on the ground floor of their house, between the theater and the bunk room. Its broad windows looked out over the lake, and its walls were lined with mirrors. He knew his dad spent an hour or so down here several days a week, but this was the first time they'd been together there in a while. So when his dad began using the same dinky clinky dumbbells as him, it dropped another gut bomb in his stomach. Worse yet was trying not to look as his dad struggled and strained.

While catching their breath between sets, Ben asked, "You like church?"

155

His dad lifted the shirt from his belly and wiped the sweat from his face. "I like it, yeah."

"How come you don't make Raymond and Rich go anymore?"

His dad sat down on the bench press machine. "They're adults. I just want you kids to know what's out there. Then when you're grown up, you can make your own decisions."

"But you want them to go?"

"I'd be happy if they went, if they believed what I believe, yes. But you can't make people believe what you believe, and Jesus said, 'Judge not, lest ye be judged.'"

"Like what you said to the team about being nice to people who are different than you, not judging them." The look of approval on his dad's face made Ben feel like he'd thrown a touchdown pass.

"Yeah, Bo. You got it."

Ben had lots of questions, but there was one thing that bothered him more than the rest. "Raymond says he doesn't go to church because more people were killed and tortured because of religion than any other reason."

His dad nodded and began pressing the weight on his machine. When he finished, he spent a good minute catching his breath. "Raymond's not wrong, but things don't need to be that way. Jesus only asked us to do two things, love God and love our neighbors as we love ourselves. He didn't say love our Christian neighbors or love our Jewish neighbors, he said our neighbors, that means *everyone*. It's men who twist things around. It's evil."

"That makes sense."

They finished their workout and spent the rest of their day off with everyone at the lake.

By five thirty, the shadows began to lengthen and the last boats could be seen heading for home. They were packing up when Torin Bennett and his dad pulled up to the dock on their way to their mooring at the country club. Everyone waved and said hello before heading up to the house. Only Ben and the coaching staff remained.

They talked about the season and how good the team was looking until Mr. Bennett removed his sunglasses and gazed at Ben's dad with a serious expression. "John, I've got to ask you because everyone is asking me. Are you okay?"

Ben's brothers stiffened, but his dad wore an easy smile. "What do you mean?"

His dad's reply obviously flustered Mr. Bennett. "Well, um, you know. The cane. The way you talk."

Ben's dad dismissed it with the wave of his hand. "Just old football injuries. Nothing, really. My back and knees and too many concussions."

Ben could tell that Mr. Bennett wanted to say more, to ask more questions, but his dad's smile was so big and so wide that there was nothing more anyone could say.

"Okay, well, that's good to hear. I mean, I'm sorry you have to deal with all that, but I'm glad it's nothing more serious." Mr. Bennett put on his glasses and started his engine.

"Just the price you have to pay." Ben's dad waved his cane in the air.

His smile lasted until the Bennett's boat was no more than a toy in the distance. "Dinner."

The three brothers followed him up the steps and the inclined concrete walkway until the halfway point, where a wrought-iron bench sat on a brick bed amid the ground cover and the towering trees. No one seemed surprised that their dad couldn't make it up in one try. He braced his hands on his knees. His head bowed as he tried to hide that he was gasping for air.

They stood around him in silence, until Rich said, "Dad, you can't keep doing that."

"Doin' what?"

Rich shook his head. "Dad, I know you don't want anyone to feel sorry for you, but people are going to speculate and make a bigger deal out of it than you want it to be."

Their father looked up with a scowl. "People can think what they want."

"Exactly." Rich got excited. "They will think what they want, unless you tell them what to think."

Raymond said, "What are you talking about?"

Rich didn't take his eyes off their dad. "Go public, Dad. You've got ALS, but you're doing what you always do. You fight. We'll do a big fundraiser, raise some money for research, tell everyone we're not moping around, letting this beat us. We're gonna beat *it*."

"How do I go public? You want me to call a press conference or something?" Their dad was still scowling.

Rich was on a roll, though, pacing back and forth on the concrete path, hands flying through the evening air. "Dad, you have friends and teammates—Deion, Favre, Goldberg, Joe Buck, Kenny Albert. Doesn't Jon Frankel work for HBO *Real*

Sports? Call everyone. Ask for contacts and ideas. Then *you* control the story. It's not a sad story. It's an *inspirational* story. It's the story of a battle, and we're not gonna lose!"

"Ya know, Stu knows Steve Kroft," Ben's dad said, clearly thinking more seriously about this.

What surprised Ben even more was the excitement lighting up Raymond's face. "The correspondent from *60 Minutes?* That would be killer."

Now Ben got excited too.

Rich finally planted his feet right in front of their dad, but his hands were still on the loose. "Yeah, Dad, you got this from playing football, but you're not bitter. You love football. You *coach* football. And you're working and writing. You're not letting this slow you down at all. This is a good plan."

"I'll contact Steve tomorrow," Ben's dad said, nodding.

The following week, at dinner before practice, Ben's dad took a sip of red wine and went into a fit of coughing. They had all grown used to this over the past several weeks during dinner. Everyone waited politely for the fit to pass. Their dad got upset if anyone made a fuss.

Finally he cleared his throat. "So I have some news. I spoke with Steve Kroft this afternoon, and *60 Minutes* is coming in three weeks to shoot the story."

Everyone went crazy.

"And they want to be here for a game." Ben's dad grinned. "So get ready for your national network debut, Bo."

That evening at practice, the excitement of being on *60 Minutes* fueled Ben's enthusiasm. He ached for perfection on every play, and not just for himself.

"Tuna, you can't give Logan the inside rush lane. You gotta protect my blind side, dude. He flattened me!"

"Finn, you're faster than that. I know you're the third receiver in the progression but run it like you're gonna score!"

Every play, Ben had notes and comments on how to make it better.

"My bad, Malik. I'll put that out in front of you on Sunday!"

"Damon, if you don't sell the fake, we're gonna get nothing on that play!"

"Thea, if you think Rohan is big, wait till you see the hogs they got at Jordan Elbridge. They will be enormous!"

"That's my bad, Woody. I can't throw it that hard. That was stupid!"

The closer they got to opening day, the more wired Ben got.

On Saturday night, he tossed and turned until his sheets were a damp tangled straitjacket. He broke free and escaped to the theater room, where Rich sat in a pod of flickering blue light. Controller in hand and headphones clamped over his ears, Rich had no notion of Ben's approach. So when he placed a finger on his brother's arm, Rich jumped out of his seat, whipped off his headset, and yelled at Ben.

"What are you doing?! You almost gave me a heart attack! You can't sneak up on a guy at . . ." Rich looked at his watch. "Two in the morning? What are you doing up? We got a game tomorrow. Today!"

"I called your name. I can't sleep, Rich, but I gotta sleep."

Rich nodded, and his tone softened. "It's okay, Bo. Calm down. You'll make it worse. It happens. I never could get to sleep the night before a game."

Ben was on the verge of tears. "You couldn't?"

"Nope, never."

"You were undefeated. You were all-state." There had to be a secret.

"Remember Dad always tells that story about training camp in the NFL one year where he was so uptight that he didn't sleep for three days straight. And that was in the old days when they practiced three times a day and went live in practice, just like a game. Finally, the team doctor gave him some heavy-duty sleeping pills."

"Uh, I don't want a sleeping pill." What if it made him sleepy for the game?

"Nah, I found something that put me to sleep. Guaranteed."

"Not . . . sleeping pills?"

161

Rich stared at him. "What? No. This."

Ben gaped at the Xbox controller that Rich held up for him to see. "You play Xbox?"

"Until I fall asleep. Zonk. Right on the couch. Try it." Rich handed him a controller.

"What about Mom and Dad?"

Rich smiled. "I got you covered."

Ben didn't know how long they played, but the next thing he knew, sunshine flooded the room waking him from a pleasant dream of victory. Rich must have placed a blanket over him and gone upstairs. Despite the dream, nervousness crawled all over his skin like a million ants.

He took a few deep breaths before getting off the couch and heading upstairs for breakfast.

By the time they got to the field, fat white clouds nearly

filled a powder-blue sky. The slightest of chills clung to the shadows where the grass was heavy with dew. The breeze promised warmer air to come, but none of the scalding summer heat Ben had grown used to. It was a perfect day for football.

Ben stepped onto the turf field where the high school team had claimed a victory Friday night under the lights. He shivered as he buckled his helmet and jogged to the twenty-yard line, joining Thea and the other early birds in a haphazard warm-up. Raymond carried their dad's director's chair to the far sideline. Rich walked slowly alongside their dad, leaving him in his chair before making a beeline for Ben.

"Did you two get in twenty snaps like I said?" Rich asked.

"Twenty-five," Thea said.

"Great." Rich blew his whistle and warm-ups began for real.

Ben couldn't keep his eyes from straying to the Jordan Elbridge side of the field. It was like picking a scab. He knew he shouldn't do it, but once he started, he just couldn't stop. Ben's team, with their gold helmets and jerseys, looked like the smart little figurines you'd find atop some little league trophy. By comparison, JE's white jerseys and pants with dark blue numbers and helmets somehow reminded Ben of prison inmates. The players were enormous, and when they began to chant, Ben couldn't help but remember last year.

JE was their only loss besides Penn Yan. Their defensive line came pouring through every single play. There had been no place for Ben to run, and when they tried to give Malik the ball, he got smashed behind the line on nearly every play. JE's offense wasn't fancy, and Ben remembered clearly his dad's praise for JE's coaching staff for their formidable game plan.

They went up and down the field four yards at a time behind their powerful O line, eating the clock, and scoring enough to win a 12–6 game.

"Big day today, Bo. You ready?" Raymond chewed a wad of gum as he wove in and out of the team as they spread out for stretching.

Ben squinted up at him from his hamstring stretch on the warm turf. "I'm ready. How's that 92 defense gonna be?"

"We'll know in about half an hour, won't we?" Raymond kept going. He'd done nothing to build Ben's confidence. If anything, he made the heavy swaying motion in Ben's stomach worse.

Time was no friend to Ben. When he wanted it to go fast, like in Mrs. Harmony's home ec class, it went slow. When he wanted it to go slow, like now when he needed more time to get mentally ready, it went fast, like lightning. Introductions were a blur. The coin flip was a snap. The kickoff was a blink.

Ben found himself suddenly four yards behind Thea, beginning the cadence. The taste of vomit reminded him that he'd thrown up behind the bench. The queasy feeling remained. The packed stands didn't help.

Rich's plan was to get Ben outside the pocket to throw the ball. The ball was in his hands before he knew it. He handled it like a hot piece of toast, then got a grip, but time was money. It only took the JE outside linebacker that missed half step by Ben to blow through Woody and Torin and beat Ben to the edge of the pocket and stop him from rolling out.

The linebacker was taller than Ben, but lanky like Rohan. Ben turned to run the other way, but the linebacker already had the momentum, and he dragged Ben down from behind like a cheetah. As he went down, Ben felt the ball being clawed from his grip. The ball spilled to the ground, covered by a pile of JE defenders.

It was a nightmare come true.

The three refs crowded the pile, peeling back the buffalo-sized defensive linemen to get to the bottom. Ben climbed slowly to his feet. To his great surprise, at the bottom of the pile was a skinny golden player curled around the football. Ben's heart swelled with relief as Thea held the ball in the air for the refs to see. He hugged her and patted the back of her helmet.

"You saved my bacon."

"Bacon?" She shoved him away.

"You know what I mean."

They'd lost thirteen yards on the play, making it second and twenty-three. Ben's teammates milled about in a state of shock over the size, strength, and quickness of their opponents.

He clapped his hands like gunshots. "Let's go! Let's go! On the ball!" Ben barked with the authority of one of his big brothers, and his teammates snapped into place.

Ben, like the rest of the offense, looked to the sideline where Mr. Moreland held up the board that among the many images was one of Allen Iverson in his Sixers jersey number three. Ben looked over at Damon. Damon saw and gave Ben a low-key nod. Now Ben looked pointedly at Finn in order not to give the defense a tip-off. Thea was down with both hands on the ball. Ben began the cadence, setting the line and taking the snap.

This time Ben snatched up the ball as he was already turning his body to go. He beat the outside linebacker to the edge by a hair. Malik released on a pass route to freeze the secondary. Likewise, Finn ran a deep post to draw his cornerback as well as the free safety away from the play. Running at top speed, Ben could see the entire defense revolving like a time-lapsed thunderstorm, ready to gobble him up.

Damon ran straight into the cornerback opposite him, then disappeared, running toward Ben. Ben handed the ball off the instant Damon passed behind him and kept running like he still had the ball. The secondary swallowed Ben's fake, hook, line, and sinker. Ben could feel the touchdown coming. The entire left side of the field was beautifully empty. He giggled to himself beneath his face mask.

Then the sharp cry of a whistle sounded, confusing Ben. He spun around to see that the defensive line had smothered Damon a good fifteen yards behind the line. They were now dangerously close to their own end zone with only a yard or two between them and a two-point safety for JE. The defense jumped for joy, high-fiving and pounding on each other's shoulder pads. They could obviously smell two points.

When Ben got back to his teammates, Thea had the line in

a loose huddle. She was on fire. "Are we gonna just poop our pants all day long? Are you guys *afraid*? Yeah, they're big! But we're as tough as they are if we let ourselves be! Tuna, you smash that number seventy-one and stop him from yakkin'. Ro, you and me are gonna double team that big oaf ninety-nine, and we *will* stop him. Jake and Omar, you guys are better than this. Now come on you guys bring it in. 'Win' on three. One, two, three . . ."

"*WIN!*"

Thea wasn't finished.

"Woody!" she shouted, pointing fearlessly at the huge outside linebacker. "You put that bald head of yours right between that guy's numbers!"

Ben was not only impressed; he was inspired. He clapped his hands and barked at his receivers. "Let's go! Let's go! On the line!"

When he looked over at their sideline for the play, though, he couldn't believe his eyes.

High over his head, Jake's dad held up the board with Allen Iverson, play number three. It had to be a mistake. The reverse was a failure. If Damon was tackled in the backfield now, it would be two points for JE *and* they'd get the ball. Ben's team would have to kick off from the twenty-yard line, giving JE excellent field position.

Ben frantically waved his arms at Rich. Once he had his attention, he made the hand signal for a time-out. The play clock was winding down, and the board had to be a mistake.

Rich shook his head no. He rolled one hand at Ben, signaling for him to hurry up and run the play he had called. Rich was scowling hard. Ben threw his hands up, surrendering. He began his cadence, hoping that Thea's pep talk would work.

He caught the snap and rolled to his right, beating the outside backer again, only cleanly. This time the secondary didn't rotate toward him. They stayed home. Damon faked his block on the cornerback, but the defender didn't buy it and instead chased Damon, nearly disrupting the handoff. Ben carried out his fake as a matter of discipline. It fooled no one.

Thea's talk worked. The O line bent, but it didn't break. No D linemen broke through and Damon raced for the opposite sideline. The cornerback to the left had only backpedaled ten yards with Finn before passing him off to the free safety and launching himself forward to meet Damon at the line of scrimmage. The inside linebackers were also making beelines for the outside.

Both cornerbacks and the pair of inside backers made a sandwich of Damon at the line of scrimmage. Ben huffed to himself. Was his brother stupid, or just crazy? It was now fourth down and thirty-seven, an impossible situation. What they needed to do was to punt, but they couldn't. They had no punter and no punt team. Rich had read some article about a high school coach in Ohio who never punted because he supposedly had statistics that proved punting gave a team no advantage.

Well, that coach's team was probably never in a fourth-and-thirty-seven situation with their backs to the goal line. Ben fumed at his brother and wasn't surprised at all to see Allen Iverson again.

"Why not?" said Ben sarcastically, although no one could hear him. He laughed bitterly to himself. This disaster would rest squarely on Rich's shoulders, not his, or Damon's, or anyone's. Then he saw something that gave him a sliver of hope.

Rich stood beside Jake's dad with forearms crossed in a big

X. That X meant that the reverse was now a fake. Ben looked at Damon and made his own X to be sure Damon knew. The play clock was winding down. Only seven seconds remained. Ben stood two yards deep in his own end zone. He barked out the cadence, and Thea snapped the ball into his hands.

He took off to his right, the first order of business being the outside backer who jammed Torin and leaped right over Woody's attempted low block at his knees. The backer accelerated upfield. Ben was cut off from the outside unless he could get around or through the defender.

Ben chose a little of both.

He ran straight at the bigger kid, lowering his shoulder. At the instant of impact, there sounded the crack of pads; Ben saw stars and spun toward the back of the end zone. He was dangerously deep in the paint, but he had slipped past his foe without losing much speed. He raced for the sideline.

Damon had already made his third fake block in a row. His cornerback was right behind him again, greedy for another sandwich, maybe in the end zone this time. Ben sprinted straight for Damon, praying for him to carry out a good fake. Ben stuck the ball in Damon's gut, but only for the smallest fraction of time.

Ben pulled the ball out smoothly, like a veteran magician extracting a card from his sleeve. Then came the Broadway part of his show. With the football tucked against his right hip, Ben looked back at Damon and *slowed down*! If the defense bought his fake, Ben would have a clear lane and it would be a one-hundred-and-two-yard race to the far end zone.

If the defenders didn't buy the fake, when Ben turned around, he was in for a mouthful of blue helmet. His stride was just north of a walk. Damon was hunched over his imaginary ball and running for his life. Still Ben winced when he turned around. It would only take one savvy linebacker or safety to destroy him.

When Ben opened his eyes, all he saw was green.

He took off like a rocket.

In the next instant, the ruse was revealed. All eleven of the blue-and-white defenders turned in hot pursuit. The only one who really had a chance was the free safety. He had sniffed something rotten and had twenty yards of depth from the line of scrimmage. If Ben had a pencil, paper, and a protractor, he could have worked out the problem of the triangle. As it was, his best guess was a three-yard advantage to the safety. A nine-foot head start in a hundred-yard dash was a lot. Ben stretched his stride.

As he ran, he was painfully aware of the posse hot on his tail. It was only a handful of seconds before the safety closed in. Ben focused on him. The safety dove for Ben's legs. He felt the impact bow his left knee in farther than it was meant to go.

A cascade of stars lit Ben's brain.

51

Ben jammed his open palm against the top of the safety's head, driving it into the turf at the one-yard line.

He regained his balance and stepped lightly into the end zone. He then jogged over to the closest official and handed him the ball as his father had instructed the entire team to do when they score.

Then came the golden mob. Ben's teammates swarmed him with pats on his helmet, shoulder pads, and butt. Woody whooped like a maniac. Tuna trumpeted. Malik went mad. Thea, however, waited for the crowd to clear before giving him a hug.

To reward Damon for his outstanding fake, Rich called a fade route in the corner of the end zone for their PAT attempt. Damon made a leaping catch for two points, giving them an 8–0 lead. The sideline was another mob scene.

"All right! All right!" Raymond cried. "Great job, offense! Now we gotta have a great kickoff and play defense just as well! Let's go!"

In a calmer voice, Raymond asked the two players who started both ways, "Rohan, Thea, you guys good? You tired from running a hundred yards for the celebration?"

Rohan grinned, but Thea was all business. "Fatigue is a state of mind, Coach."

Ben could tell by his brother's face that Raymond loved it.

He knew Rich was equally happy with him, although his compliments were always balanced out by something you did wrong. "Bo, awesome job with your fake! For a second, I thought you didn't see the X, but then you took off. I can't believe you let that guy catch you."

"Yeah, I wanted to test out my stiff arm."

"Wise guy. Don't let Dad hear you."

"I thought you were going crazy calling the same play three times in a row," Ben said.

"Crazy like a fox." Rich pointed to his temple and winked.

Ben stopped at his father's chair on his way to the bench. "Hey, Dad."

"Hey, you. Come here and give me a hug; that was awesome!"

Ben put his arms around his dad's shoulders with his head on his chest. His dad kissed the top of his sweaty head, but the arms he had wrapped around Ben's back were weak and trembling. "That fake was a masterpiece. You had everyone fooled, and the move you put on the outside linebacker? Just spectacular."

Tears welled up in his eyes, and Ben nearly choked. "Thanks, Dad."

His dad patted his back with a feeble hand. "Do it again, Bo. Do it again."

Ben sat down on the bench between Tuna and Malik. He cracked open his bottle of orange Gatorade and took a couple swigs.

He turned to Tuna. "What?"

Tuna broke his stare. "Um . . . What was your dad saying to you? Anything about the O line?"

Ben hesitated, then realized that his dad's speech had deteriorated into mush. It was mush *he* could understand because he was around him so much. "No, Tuna. Nothing about the line."

"Because we didn't need your girlfriend's little speech to get us fired up, you know. I was just feelin' my guy out." Tuna rested his arms on his thigh pads and looked sideways at Ben. "I had his number. I buried that guy on the touchdown."

"Girlfriend?" Ben couldn't believe that junk. "What the—"

Malik shook his head. "Yeah, Tuna. Not cool, brother."

"You don't have to be embarrassed because she called you out." Ben stood to go.

"I see the way you look at her."

"Are you *crazy*?" Ben stepped back to the bench.

Tuna stood up and bumped chests.

Malik jumped between them. "Yo! You two chill! Seriously. We got a game to win."

"Yeah." Ben glared at Tuna.

"Yeah." Tuna glared right back.

Ben snorted and turned toward the field, where Raymond's 92 defense lined up for its first true test. Just like last year, JE lined up in a power-I formation with two tight ends. They meant to pound down the defense with their massive offensive line, running the ball all day long. The 92 put a man in every gap. The defense's job was to shoot through those gaps on every play.

On the very first snap, Rohan burst through the A gap, blasted the fullback, and tackled the runner behind the line of scrimmage. He jumped up and high-fived his excited teammates. That play set the tone for the day. JE had a few break-out plays, and one long touchdown drive, but otherwise the 92 defense was a dominant force. The one time JE did try to pass, Thea intercepted it and ran it back for a touchdown.

On the offensive side of the ball, Ben took some hard shots, but they scored four more touchdowns before Sol came in to get some snaps. On the sideline, Ben shook hands with everyone, even Tuna. Ben put a hand on his dad's shoulder after receiving another hug.

His dad kept a watchful eye on the field even when he spoke. "You know, John Madden always said that winning is a deodorant that takes away all bad smells."

Ben couldn't help himself from saying, "Yeah, if it works for rotten fish, I guess it works for anything."

His dad took his eyes off the field for a moment. "Do I even want to know?"

Ben laughed and shook his head. "No."

"You know," his dad said, turning his eyes back to the field, "I was worried about this one."

"They're tough."

"And big," said his dad.

"Huge." Ben loved talking with his dad like equals.

His dad took his eyes off the field again and lowered his voice. "I wouldn't say this to anyone but you, Bo, not even your brothers. But these guys are the best team we'll see by far, until Penn Yan. All we have to do is take care of business and we should crush everyone else."

"Why wouldn't you say it to anyone but me?"

"Well, it's bad luck to say it, but I'm hoping it will help you keep your breakfast in your stomach."

Nice as it was of his dad to try and take some pressure off of Ben after the win, it didn't work. Ben threw up before the next three games. Woody decided this was good luck for the team, and he began taking bets on how many minutes before kickoff that Ben would blow chunks. School began, and it seemed the entire sixth grade was taking bets. While embarrassing, the interest in the team exploded, and the stands at home games overflowed.

His dad was right about the teams they faced after Jordan Elbridge. They rolled them up like cheap rugs. Ben threw touchdown after touchdown. Some of the kids called him Ben Brady in the hallways at school.

So the entire team was riding high when the *60 Minutes* crew showed up one day at the Friday-evening practice, giving everyone an added shot of adrenaline.

Tuna grabbed Woody at the beginning of their first water break. "I got thirty minutes before kickoff."

Malik overheard this and grabbed Woody by the other arm. "And I'm betting on his puking the minute he gets out of the truck."

"Guys. I'm standing right here." Ben shook his head. "You're supposed to be my friends."

They all laughed.

Ben couldn't really be mad at his friends. They weren't wrong. Even the sight of the cameras at practice made him queasy. He worried now that the pressure could force him to press too hard and rob the team of what should be an easy win. How would that look on *60 Minutes*?

Practice was crisp with the exception of Ben's fumbling of several perfect snaps and misfiring on all but a few passes.

"Get it out of your system now!" Rich screamed, holding two handfuls of his own hair.

Ben's dad said nothing about the camera crew and producers, and he seemed not to notice them even when they were right up in his face. Ben and his teammates, however, stood a little straighter and ran a little faster when the cameras got anywhere near them.

Over the past couple weeks, Ben's dad had spoken less and less to the team. Raymond and Rich took over because no one except his own sons could understand him, and even they were beginning to have problems. So, Ben was surprised at the end of practice when his dad blew his whistle and stood up out of his chair.

His dad, now thinning and stooped over like someone thirty

years older, still had that fiery glint in his eyes. Two cameras rolled from different angles, one over Rohan's shoulder and one from the grass between Finn and Thea. The sound man held what Ben had heard them call a boom mic. The ten-foot pole had a brass cylinder attached to one end as a counterweight. On the end hovering a couple feet above his dad's head was a furry gray microphone looking like a super-fat squirrel's tail.

When he spoke, Ben heard his dad as the microphone heard him.

"Aw rye, gway radish gayz. Ih ee lay lie ad unnay, ee onna win annona un. En? Oo dakum don."

He knew right away that "En" meant Ben because his dad looked straight at him. And he knew "dakum don" meant to break them down partly because that's the way they always ended practice. Ben jumped to the middle of the team and looked around the loose circle. The squirrel tail leaped to the space above his head, and the cameras kept rolling. Legs pumped like pistons in a way they never had before. When he broke them down, the unified war cry nearly split his eardrums.

On the truck ride home, Rich stopped and looked over at their father sitting in the passenger seat. "So I told the producer, Draggan, that we should do the interview with Steve around two. That'll give you time to get up and shower and have breakfast in case you sleep late."

Their dad read in bed every night, usually until around midnight. As his ALS progressed, it became harder and harder to breathe, and his oxygen count was low. Therefore, he typically slept eleven and sometimes twelve hours a night.

"After that," Rich continued, "they want to get some shots of the family all in the boat out on the lake and then of you and Steve walking in town." The light turned green, and Rich glanced back at Ben before making the turn.

"Then Sunday, it's *show*time."

53

Later the next day, Ben walked into the living room, which was a mess with all kinds of tech.

Cables lay everywhere, twisted about the floor like a spilled spaghetti dinner. Suitcase-sized lights mounted on tripods painted the room with soft yellow light. There were two cameras again, this time mounted atop tripods so heavy they looked like engines of war. Ben recognized everyone from the night before. Cameramen, audio technicians, and Draggan, the producer, with his blonde assistant.

Only now, there were twice as many people. A makeup artist applied her wares to his dad while a hair stylist fussed with the graying locks on his forehead. Assistants stood behind half the people. Two more held giant circular reflectors that cast the light back up into Steve's and his dad's faces. Steve also had an assistant who had a notepad and a pen in constant motion.

Ben's family stood crowded into the kitchen, whispering among themselves. His mom peppered Draggan's assistant with questions. Ben sat in one of the green leather chairs around the table. He stared down at the lake, where the wooded hills were beginning to fade from green to yellow, orange, red, and finally brown before leaving the trees barren and lifeless in just a few weeks' time.

It was beautiful, really, but it would be gone in a matter of weeks. Too short for Ben. An ugly thought crept into his mind. Wasn't his dad like the trees? Tall and majestic, his mom would say beautiful, but quickly fading. Week by week. Day by day. Minute by minute? A small groan escaped from his chest.

"Shh!" Raymond pressed a finger to his lips and motioned his head toward the living room.

Ben could barely see his dad through all the people and equipment, but the host of *60 Minutes*, Steve Kroft, was talking.

Then he heard his dad's voice, deep like Steve's, but slurred so badly that Ben wondered how anyone could understand. The longer the interview went, the more painful it was. Ben stood and moved in front of Rich, who put his hands on Ben's shoulders and gave them a squeeze. From there Ben could see his dad clearly, bathed in the gentle light. His hair never seemed so gray or his face so aged.

Ben didn't hear the question Steve Kroft asked his dad, but when his face crumpled and tears welled up in his eyes, Ben cringed. With his senses sharpened, he listened carefully to his dad. Ben suddenly realized that his dad's tears weren't from sadness or despair or self-pity. The tears streaming down his cheeks were tears of joy.

"I've never been happier." Ben's dad sniffed, and then a smile spread across his face like sunshine. "I have my faith and my family all around me. I'm blessed."

The interview lasted for more than an hour before the family and the cameras and Draggan walked down the path to the lake. Sunlight washed the trees on the hillsides so that the many colors shone rich and bright. The sky was powder blue with a great smear of distant white on the horizon and small flattened puffs atop the hills. The family piled into the big blue boat and took off down the lake. Wind whipped his dad's hair, and the pure joy on his face made him look suddenly ten years younger.

Behind them was their home, perched high up on the bluff. His dad never apologized for the large house, saying he had paid for it with his blood and bones. During the interview, Ben was somewhat amazed that his dad bore the NFL and the game itself no ill will. He was very clear that his doctors blamed his condition on the game and the head traumas that came with it.

Ben thought about his mom's words about football, and also what Rich had said. Meanwhile, his dad and Raymond had the opposite opinions about football. That put Ben in the middle. He had to weigh the stress of the game versus the glory and thrill of scoring touchdowns. Then there were the injuries. His dad might be happy, but Ben feared his dad's fate more than anything he could think of.

When they returned to the dock, Ben hung back with his dad, who slowly climbed the path. The older kids had plans to go apple-picking, and his mom was in some deep discussion with Draggan. His dad put a hand on Ben's shoulder and pulled him close.

"I love you, Bo."

"Love you too, Dad."

"And I'm really proud of you. Not because you're a great football player, but because you are a great kid." They were halfway up the path, and his dad reached for the bench, stumbled, and fell to his knees on the concrete.

"Dad!" Ben scrambled to help him up and find a seat on the bench.

He felt tears filling his eyes, but his dad brushed at the scuff marks on the knees of his jeans. "I'm okay. I'm fine."

They sat quietly for a moment, and Ben fought back the tears. He didn't know if his dad had seen them or not.

"You know, I don't care if you play football or not. It's only if you want to play, I am not gonna let your mom stop you."

"Can you do that?" Ben's mom was half the size of his dad, but she was a force.

"Yeah. I can, and I will. You just let me know."

54

The air, crisp like a bite of fresh apple, hinted of the winter to come. The sun was like an egg yolk in the clear blue sky. It was a glorious Sunday for football. As they pulled into the parking lot Ben saw the cameras, the producer Draggan, and the *60 Minutes* crew. Smells from the concession stand, hot dogs and burgers on the grill, greeted Ben's nose the moment he opened the truck door.

It smelled like game day, but Ben gulped back the bile from his stomach. He could hear Woody collecting bets. He walked tall across the blacktop. His cleats clacked on the concrete steps, and he made it to the turf, where he pointed, smiling at Malik. Word had reached him of an eighty-five-dollar pot, seventeen teammates betting five dollars each against him keeping his breakfast off the turf.

The stadium clock said 38:54. He had to hang on for nine

more minutes to ruin Tuna's chance at the pot. He didn't forget the bets his two friends made right in front of him. If he had his way, neither would win, but his stomach convulsed as one of the cameramen rushed over for a shot of the head coach and his three sons making their entrance.

Ben tugged on his helmet and jogged across the field, leaving his brothers and dad behind. He pulled a ball from the bag Mr. Bennett had brought, then grabbed Thea. From the forty-yard line, he handled Thea's snaps, pump-faked left, and performed a three-step drop. He'd done no more than two before Finn and Damon appeared and ran the hitch and go route that went with Ben's action.

Soon, Torin, Woody, and Malik joined the line to loosen their legs while Ben loosened his arm. Wolcott, the opposing team, was doing the same. When the clock turned to 29:59, Ben shouted at Tuna in the end zone and jabbed his finger toward the scoreboard. Tuna showed Ben his enormous butt and slapped it several times to everyone's delight. Sol joined in. Tuna snapped to him while the receivers mixed in some new patterns and changed sides until Raymond blew his whistle to begin some dynamic stretching.

After stretching, the skill players ran seven-on-seven while the linemen battered each other in the end zone. After ten minutes of teamwork, they headed to the back of the end zone for introductions. The stands were full of fans spilling over to the grass hillside. Pressure mounted inside Ben's head and stomach. He couldn't tell which was worse.

When the announcer called Ben's name and number, he sprinted through the two lines of cheerleaders. Waiting for him at the forty-yard line were his two brothers and the three team-mates with numbers less than his own number seven, the same number Rich had broken numerous records in during his all-state season. He gave high fives to everyone, then took his place on the forty, gulping down the stomach juices that continued to flow the wrong way.

Once the whole team had been introduced, Raymond had Rohan take the center of the team to break them down. Ben swore he felt like an ancient warrior before battle. He was so pumped up, he now felt certain that breakfast was his. When he hit the sideline, he gave his dad a high five.

"Get 'em, Bo." His dad slapped his helmet.

When Ben peeled away from his dad, the cameras were on him like flies. Ben retreated to behind the bench, but they followed. Mercifully, the announcer asked everyone to stand and remove their hats for the national anthem. Ben escaped to the sideline, helmet off, in a straight row with his team. He had just breathed a sigh of relief when he saw one camera round the end of the line, take the field, and begin to close in on him.

He thought about how badly he'd practiced on Friday. His confidence crumbled. How many times had his dad quoted the famous college coach George O'Leary? "You practice how you play." The cameras would be locked on him during the game, and if he played how he practiced, the game would be a disaster. Would Rich pull him for Sol if things got bad? Anything was possible if he stood between Rich and winning.

The anthem ended.

Ben left his helmet off and dashed behind the bench. He couldn't have a big splat of vomit on the turf for the world to see. The trash barrel was too far. He couldn't barf on himself either. Under the bench sat the duffel bag Tuna brought to each game to store extra contact lenses, Gatorade, and the lucky padded gloves he wore only for games.

Ben waved the cameras off, dropped to his knees, and puked in Tuna's duffel bag.

55

Tuna shrieked loud enough to raise the dead. "What the—"

Thea appeared, laughing hysterically.

"Not funny! Not funny *at all*!" Tuna's face burned from pink to red.

Ben wiped his mouth on the back of his hand and looked up, shamefaced. "Sorry."

Fortunately, Thea continued to distract Tuna with her laughter, only now she pointed toward the scoreboard. "Look! I won! Eighty-five smackers! I bet game time, and you laughed at me. Who's laughing now? HA!"

They played twelve-minute quarters, and the clock on the scoreboard read 12:00. It was game time.

"My gloves!" Tuna whined. "My lucky gloves!"

"Stop whimpering and clean them off. Here, I'll do it." Thea reached into the bag and removed the soiled gloves. She made a squeegee of her forefinger and began to sweep the vomit onto the turf.

"Aww! That stinks!"

"These aren't so bad. You've never been in a cow barn. Smell." Thea thrust a glove under Tuna's nose.

Tuna gagged, choked, dropped to his own knees, and barfed up a yellow puddle studded with chunks of what may have been sausage.

Thea looked with interest. "You know, you shouldn't be eating sausage before a game. It doesn't digest well. Look."

Ben turned away with a heave, bringing up nothing of interest.

Rich appeared. "What in the world?"

"Don't worry, Coach. They're fine. Just the jitters." Thea pulled her helmet on and snapped it up.

"Well, we won the toss, so let's go." Rich turned and walked away.

Ben was relieved that the cameras had disappeared. "Sorry, Tuna. Really. I'll get you new ones."

Thea put a hand on Tuna's shoulder. "Based on your reaction, maybe you could use these things as, like, weapons."

Tuna stood and stalked away without a word. Thea offered Ben a hand and helped him up.

Ben suddenly felt embarrassed. "Thanks."

"Come on. Let's go thrash these guys."

Ben felt mildly ashamed that he had to be propped up by Thea. Not because she was a girl, but as the quarterback, he felt he should be a better leader. So he strapped up his own helmet and took the field.

On the first play Ben fumbled the snap. Luckily, the ball didn't go too far and he was able to dive on it before being buried under a pile of Wolcott defenders. The refs cleared the pile, and against his will, Ben's eyes were drawn to his brother. Rich was having a tantrum on the sideline.

"Come *on*!" Rich's shout could be heard in the next town over.

The offense lined up, and Ben got into position. Jake's dad held up the board that included a picture of Michael Vick. Play number seven. The bubble screen, a short pass to Malik with Woody and Torin as blockers. Ben looked around. Everyone was in the right place.

He barked out the cadence and took the snap. He threw a miserable pass to Malik, right at his ankles. Malik miraculously grabbed it and banged through two defenders before being brought down at the original line of scrimmage. The next play, a hitch pass to Finn, Ben threw over his head. On fourth down, Ben fumbled on the handoff to Damon on the reverse.

The offense jogged off the field, heads hung low.

The Wolcott defense went crazy, jumping and whooping and high-fiving their offense as it poured onto the field. Five plays later, Wolcott found the end zone. In the stands, the smaller Wolcott crowd made enough noise to fill a college stadium. On Ben's sideline, the *60 Minutes* cameras continued to roll.

By halftime Wolcott led 20–6.

The team gathered in the end zone, drinking Gatorade and sucking on orange wedges. Their coaches stood huddled around Ben's dad. Finally they broke and marched toward the end zone, Ben's dad among them talking to Raymond. The cameramen, along with Draggan and two sound techs took a break on the bench.

Rich went over the troubles with the offense, placing the blame squarely on Ben's shoulders without directly naming him.

"We're not making any changes. Yet." Rich leveled his gaze on Ben as if they were the only two people there.

Raymond addressed the defense, ending with praise for Thea, who accounted for their only touchdown with a pick six. "We need more big plays like that on defense. I want everyone going for the ball. We need more turnovers. Our offense is struggling today, so we have to pick up the slack."

Ben took that as another dig at him. He was having a terrible day. Didn't that happen to even the best athletes sometimes? Ben sat with his back against the goalpost. He dropped his head between his knees. When everyone rose to head to the bench for the second half, Ben remained.

A shadow fell over him.

Ben looked up. His dad smiled down on him, subbing in for the sun.

"I'm sorry, Dad."

"You have nothing to be sorry for." His dad looked like he really meant it.

"But, *60 Minutes.*"

His dad waved an impatient hand. "That doesn't matter."

"No?"

"What matters is this. We have five and a half games left together, and I want you to enjoy every minute. I'm going to.

194

This is the last football season I'll ever coach."

Ben shivered as a chill raced down his spine.

"Nothing to be upset about, Bo." His dad offered a hand and pulled Ben to his feet. "You mind letting an old man lean on you?"

Ben shook his head. "You're not old."

"Tell that to my back and knees." His dad laughed, and they began to walk.

His dad hadn't been kidding. He leaned on Ben, nearly tipping him over. Ben recovered and stood strong. He helped him all the way to his chair.

His dad sat with a quiet groan. "I do want you to do one thing out there for me, okay? Can you do it?"

Ben nodded. "Okay."

His dad broke into a wide smile. "Just have fun."

56

They began on defense.

Raymond dialed up some blitzes and line stunts. The first play was a sweep to Luke Logan's side. The offensive tackle had a good hold of his jersey, but he spun and swiped at the running backs legs like a big cat, dropping him four yards behind the line. Now it was time for Skaneateles to celebrate.

The next play, Wolcott's quarterback dropped back to pass. Rohan and Torin had an X stunt on. Torin crashed down, and Rohan looped around, blew up the fullback, and sacked the quarterback for a seven-yard loss. The next play was a screen pass that Johnny Congel chased down for a gain of only two.

The defense went wild, jumping and screaming and banging face masks with their offense counterparts, shouting, *"Let's go!"*

Wolcott's punter squibbed it, and the ball landed out of

bounds on their own forty-two-yard line. Ben charged the field with his offense close behind. When he saw the Allen Iverson play, he pumped his fist. His father's words had set him free. He took the snap and rolled right. Someone missed a block and a linebacker came shooting toward him.

The Wolcott player closed the distance in a blink, but he came in high and Ben used his stiff arm, thrusting his palm into the backer's chest like a punch. The defender went down like a duck in a shooting gallery. When he looked up, Damon was nearly upon him, and Ben felt a stab of panic. Damon was early and he was late.

If he fumbled this, he felt certain Rich would pull him for Sol. Despite his dad's words about fun, he knew he couldn't mess this up. He needed to make a clean handoff, and that required both hands; that was the rule. Well, sometimes you had to break the rules.

Ben had the point of the ball in his palm, trapping it in the crook of his elbow. He squeezed the point with all his might and extended his arm, tucking the ball in Damon's breadbasket as he went speeding by. Ben finished the play with a fake that had the cornerback trying to tackle him. Ben disposed of him with another stiff arm, feeding him a turf sandwich.

Damon ran for thirty-five yards. To slow down the defense's pass rush, Rich called a freeze play. Ben's linemen whispered "Ice" to each other, and Ben barked out a hard count worthy of Tom Brady. The entire Wolcott defensive line jumped offsides, giving Ben's team a free five yards, and slowing down the Wolcott D line. Three plays later, Malik scored on a bubble screen pass from Ben. Finn ran a crossing route in the end zone for a two-point conversion and suddenly Skaneateles was right back in the game trailing only 14–20.

With a revved-up defense and Ben playing like he usually did, they soon had a twenty-two-point lead. Ben had four passing touchdowns, and he walked tall in front of the *60 Minutes* cameras. Raymond put all the reserves in on defense to give them as much playing time as possible. Wolcott took advantage and scored a touchdown and a two-point conversion, closing the gap 28–42.

The fourth quarter had just begun.

On the sideline Rich talked quietly with Draggan; then he put his arm around Ben's shoulders. "Draggan wants to know if I can call a running play where you can score."

Ben nodded. "And?"

"So the first play is gonna be the reverse X. They're gonna set up the cameras on the sideline to get the perfect shot. They want to make it part of the piece."

Excitement flooded Ben's frame. He could just imagine seeing himself running for a touchdown on TV with millions of people watching.

All he had to do now was make the play.

Ben whispered to Damon. "We're running the reverse, but I'm keeping it. Give me a good fake, man. The cameras will be on me."

Damon grinned and slapped his shoulder pad. He had already run three reverses in the game, one for a touchdown. With a good fake and Ben's speed, the play had a good chance to score.

The kickoff took a twisted bounce and slipped through the Skaneateles return team. Malik made a smart play by diving on the ball, but Ben would have to run seventy-one yards to score. He lined up behind Thea and saw Jake's dad with the Allen Iverson board. No one but Damon and Ben knew about the fake. Rich wanted to insure everyone blocked it like a reverse so the defense would buy it completely.

Ben called out the cadence, took the snap, and ran toward

Damon. Ben faked the handoff to Damon but was too excited to slow down. The cornerback covering Damon wasn't fooled, but when he tried to tackle Ben, Ben lowered his shoulder and blasted him. The rest of the defense sniffed out the fake and turned in pursuit of Ben.

Ben ignited the jets, leaving them in his dust.

They won the Wolcott game 50–34.

The week flew by, with homework and practice taking up all of Ben's time. Ben noticed his dad not feeling well, but anytime he asked him about it, his dad brushed it off with a laugh. That weekend, they went to East Rochester and easily won that game 42–14. When they got home that evening, *60 Minutes* began at 8:00 p.m. on CBS after the Patriots versus Chiefs game. Ben and his family, sister, brothers, and significant others gathered around the TV to watch. The only one missing was his sister Rosie, who had returned to Harvard.

Ben seemed to be the only nervous one. His dad wore an easy smile. His brothers joked about who besides their dad would get the most face time.

"We may as well stop arguing about it," said Rich. "We both know who's gonna win."

"Yeah," Raymond said with a smirk. "Bo."

Everyone laughed except Ben. He forced a smile and wondered if Thea would be watching.

Ben swelled with pride as the host, Steve Kroft, remembered his dad's career with the Atlanta Falcons well before his existence. They showed highlights of his dad, formidable and ferocious, sacking legends like Favre, Elway, Montana, and

Moon, and tackling Barry Sanders and Herschel Walker. They talked about a book his dad wrote about life in the NFL, some TV work, and his law degree. Then the story turned dark.

ALS was explained as a fatal disease with horrible symptoms and no cure. Football, his dad said, was a game he loved. They showed him coaching with Ben's brothers, and then they talked about Ben. They showed his touchdown run. His family all cheered, and his brothers slapped his back. The piece ended with a sliver of hope, his dad's fundraising efforts and the research his doctor, Dr. Sucovich, and her team were doing at Mass General. Finally, his dad talked tearfully about the rich life he'd had and how this time in his life was happier than he'd ever been before, despite his ALS diagnosis.

Ben had tears in his eyes, but he glanced at his mom and dad, brothers and sister, and he saw that he wasn't alone.

Afterward, they all watched a football movie, *Remember the Titans*. Ben felt exhausted. It had been a long, and good, day. As good as the movie was, he fell asleep sitting on the couch.

The next thing he knew, his dad was shaking him awake. "Come on, Bo. You had a big day."

He sat up and rubbed one eye. "What happened at the end of the movie? Did they win?"

"Sure you don't want to watch it tomorrow?"

"No, just tell me." Ben yawned.

"They did. It's a true story."

Ben got up. "Good."

Up the stairs, he made his way to his room and fell into bed. He immediately fell asleep again.

Then Ben felt someone yank him from the deep darkness of

his dreamless sleep. He cringed when a light pierced through to the center of his foggy brain. "Hey, Ben." Rich shook his arm. "Get up."

"Stop!" Ben cried.

"Ben, wake up! Dad can't breathe. We're taking him to the hospital."

58

A chill gripped Ben in the third row of seats in his mom's big SUV. Raymond shocked them all by carrying their dad like a sack of concrete to the truck. Rich had a white-knuckle hold on the wheel as they hurtled through the darkness. Ben's dad sat next to Rich in a reclined seat that put him in their mom's lap. She stroked his face while he gasped for air like one of the fish caught in Tuna's boathouse flopping on the concrete. Ben didn't think he was conscious.

Tension ruled them all. Raymond sat in profound silence next to their mom, with Cara beside him. Jessica sat beside Ben. He wanted to ask her the dozens of questions rattling inside his head. She was the nurse and the family's authority on health issues, but the lines of worry creasing her pretty face warned him away from any questions.

Holding a phone to her ear with her free hand, Ben's mom

had their family doctor on the line making emergency arrangements for their arrival at the hospital.

She said thank you and goodbye before hanging up. "Dr. Cohen said to pull up to the main entrance and they'll take him right to the ICU. Do you know the main entrance, Rich?"

"Yeah, Mom. That's where I drop off Jessica sometimes."

Their mom nodded, stroking their dad's face all the while.

When they arrived, two orderlies rushed to the truck, removed their dad, and whisked him away on a stretcher. A doctor covered his face with an oxygen mask and ran along one side of the stretcher as their mom ran along the other.

When Rich turned around in his seat, his pale face frightened Ben. "Raymond, you and Cara can take Ben. Jessica and I will park and meet you."

They sat tightly grouped in a waiting room. Ghostly calls for doctors on intercoms echoed through the empty halls. Ben stared at a big round-faced clock on the wall. The red second hand crawled past the numbers, painfully slow. The black minute hand lay frozen, and the hour hand was locked in granite.

Ben must have dozed off because suddenly his mom appeared with a female doctor in a white coat wearing a frown.

"How is he?" Rich asked as the doctor and their mom sat.

"It's pneumonia," their mom said.

The doctor nodded.

"Pneumonia?" Raymond looked up from his private thoughts. "He was fine all day, all week. How can he suddenly just have pneumonia?"

Ben remembered his dad had looked a little off earlier, but he didn't think anything like this would ever happen.

"Your father is a strong man." The doctor bit her lip. "The problem is his level of carbon dioxide. Right now he's at eighty-four. He's delirious, but most people lose consciousness at eighty. Normal is around thirty. At ninety the heart stops."

"What can we do?" Rich jumped up from his seat. He always believed there was something you could do.

"We can give him a tracheotomy," said the doctor. "That would allow us to put him on a ventilator and help to clear his lungs, flush them with saline, then suction them out, hopefully helping to clear the infection and the fluid buildup. Right now he's not cooperating. He keeps trying to leave."

Rich wore a mask of horror, and his voice dropped. "Dad told me once that he never wanted a tracheotomy, that if he got to that point to just let him go."

"Rich, come on," Raymond said. Their mom just looked down and shook her head.

Ben couldn't believe what Rich was saying was true. His dad never talked about quitting in anything. How could he simply quit on his own life? How could he quit on *him*? Tears of anger and despair flooded Ben's eyes.

He leaped out of his seat. "No!"

Everyone turned to stare.

"Ben, honey." Ben's mom broke the uncomfortable silence. "No, Dad never quits on anything." She paused and looked at Ben's brothers. "You go in, Raymond, Rich. You talk to him. Bring Ben. He needs a dad."

"Okay, Mom. Come on, Bo." Rich turned to the doctor. "Can Jessica come? She's a nurse here."

"I'm in the NICU." Jessica stood up.

The doctor looked at Jessica and paused to think. "The limit is two, so I'm already stretching it, but if you're a nurse, I guess it'll work."

Ben walked along the bright hallway in a daze, trailing the rest of them.

The corridor seemed endless, but they finally found their dad's room. A monitor stood beeping quietly beside the bed. Numbers and the squiggly line tracking the rhythm of his dad's heart lit the screen. His dad's head faced the window. An oxygen tube circled his ear and poked into his nose, gently hissing.

The doctor touched his shoulder. "Mr. Redd. Your boys are here to see you."

Their dad lurched up and pawed at the tubing around his face.

Raymond placed a strong hand on his shoulder, but he spoke softly. "Dad, easy. We're here."

"Good, let's go." He stared with glassy eyes and began to try and swing his legs over the side of the bed.

"Whoa." Raymond caught them and eased them back. "Dad, you gotta stay here. They're gonna help you."

Rich manned the other side of the bed, and their dad appealed to him. "Rish, less go."

"No, Dad. Raymond's right. You need to stay. They need to give you a tracheotomy, Dad."

"Nope. I'm fine. Get me out of here. We got a game." Again, he swung his legs up over the railing, and again Raymond stopped him.

"Dad, listen to me." Rich leaned over and got right in his face. "You're going to be able to breathe so much easier. You'll get stronger. You won't feel so tired all the time. It's a good thing, okay?"

"It's good?" With a suspicious squint in his eyes, he looked from Rich to Raymond and then seemed to stare blankly at Ben.

Ben couldn't speak, but he managed to nod.

Their dad's face softened. He laid his head back into the

pillow, and he didn't struggle when Jessica straightened the oxygen tubes.

"Okay," he said. "Okay."

He closed his eyes.

Raymond turned to the doctor in a panic. "Is he all right?"

"I'll need you all to leave now. I need to get him intubated and get his CO_2 down so Dr. Kumar can operate in the morning. We'll keep him sedated. Thank you. You just saved his life." The doctor got down to business, speaking with nurses and two physician assistants in undertones. They all hurried about with obvious urgency.

Jessica squeezed Ben's shoulder and addressed his brothers. "Let's go. Your mom will want to hear."

Jessica led them down the different hallways back to the waiting room.

"What's wrong?" Ben's mom asked as she saw them.

"Nothing. It went great. Raymond and I reasoned with him, and Ben, I think, tugged at his heart strings." Rich sounded like they'd just celebrated a birthday.

Their mom scowled. "What's *wrong*, Jessica?"

Jessica's head hung low, and when she raised her chin, the moisture in her eyes glinted under the pale neon lights. "We got him to go along, yes, but no one told him . . ."

"What, Jessica?" their mom said impatiently. "No one told him what?"

A tear rolled down her cheek. "That he'll probably never talk again."

Raymond stayed with their mom at the hospital. Rich drove everyone else home. Ben lay down at seven and woke up at noon. He didn't get on Xbox, and he didn't reply to anyone's texts. Rich took him and Jessica to lunch at Doug's Fish Fry. Rich talked about the houses he and their dad owned around the university that they had turned into rental properties for student housing. Rich had big plans for expansion into apartment buildings and complexes when he finished law school, and he wanted Ben to study business in college and come work with him.

Ben nodded but remained quiet until he finished his food and said, "What about Dad?"

"Dad? Dad's gonna be great. He'll get well and get off this ventilator in no time," Rich said, almost cheerfully.

Jessica covered Rich's hand with her own. "Rich, you can't

just say it like that. Pneumonia for someone with ALS is really dangerous, and you can't expect him to get off a ventilator once he's on it."

"Jessica, you're gonna scare him," Rich whispered, nodding at Ben. "Our dad isn't a normal person."

"I'm not scared." Ben sat up straight.

"I'm just saying you have to be realistic. He's in the ICU, the intensive care unit. It's very serious," Jessica said.

"Are we having practice tomorrow?" Ben asked.

"Yeah. Why wouldn't we?" Rich gave him a puzzled look.

"Cuz Dad."

Rich laughed. "Dad? *Our* dad? He wouldn't want a practice missed on account of him. You know that."

Ben shrugged.

Later that day, Rose came home from Harvard. Ben and Rich and Jessica picked her up at the airport, and they all went straight to the hospital.

"How is he?" Ben asked the second they saw their mom.

She rubbed his head and pulled him into a hug. "Dr. Kumar said the operation went well. Dad's sleeping now. They're worried about the pneumonia. Both lungs are pretty bad, but he's strong."

"Can I see him?" Ben asked.

His mom laid her hand along his cheek. "We'll be real quiet."

Ben followed her down the hallway. They turned twice before passing through some automatic doors. At the nursing station outside his dad's room, women and men in blue and purple scrubs stood talking in whispers. Inside the room a nurse finished changing an IV bag, said a quiet hello, and left them.

The machines surrounding the bed blinked and beeped and hissed at Ben. A ribbed plastic hose fed air in and out of his dad's throat in a steady rhythm. His bloodless face looked more like death than sleep. Ben's mom ran her fingers through his hair, but his dad didn't move.

"Football did this, Benjamin." The soft, smoky sound of her voice made Ben wonder if he had imagined it.

Ben said nothing.

Everyone kept saying how his dad was strong, but lying there, pale, with IVs dripping medicine into his veins, and a machine pumping air in and out of his lungs, he didn't look so strong. Jessica's words rang in his ears. His dad had a dangerous infection in his lungs, one that could kill him. They cut a hole in his throat so a machine could breathe for him. He knew his Dad's strength, but he also knew that right now, his life depended on more than that.

At practice on Tuesday evening, Tuna greeted Ben in the parking lot. "I am so sorry about your dad, Ben."

Ben stopped in his tracks. He looked to his brothers, but they had already walked away. "Uh, thanks, Tuna. He'll be okay."

"Really? That's great to hear." Tuna's face showed genuine concern, but also doubt. "Everyone was worried when you didn't answer anyone's texts."

"How did you even know?"

"Well, everyone saw *60 Minutes*. Wow, I mean we all figured something. You know, the cane and his . . . talking, but *ALS*. And now the hospital. Man, I'm just sorry." Tuna held out a big paw, and Ben shook it.

Ben let go and headed toward the grass.

"Anything I can do." Tuna's voice chased after him, but Ben

had already pulled his helmet on and he pretended not to hear.

60 Minutes Ben could understand, but he couldn't figure how anyone, let alone *everyone*, could have heard about the hospital.

He saw Woody and Malik walking toward him with more sad faces. He wanted to shout out to everyone that his dad was a freak. He had the strength of a dinosaur and the heart of a lion, that ALS couldn't beat *him*. And *pneumonia*? A joke. Ben averted his eyes and grabbed Thea as she walked by. He jogged beside her to their usual spot in the far end zone.

He clapped his hands before she could speak and said, "Okay, let's get going. I want to get twenty snaps in before the whistle."

Thea nodded and, without a word, got into her stance and waited for his cadence. They only got in seventeen before Raymond blew his whistle, calling everyone in. When they got there, though, Rich cleared his throat to speak.

"I know some of you watched Coach on *60 Minutes* after the Chiefs game Sunday night, so you know what he's dealing with." Rich looked around like a playground bully challenging all comers. "He's not here tonight because he's in the hospital."

Raymond stared at his feet and kicked the grass with his toe.

Rich's face brightened, and he moved his hands the way you'd calm a crowd. "Now, he's gonna be fine. He's got a little pneumonia, so he may be there for a few days, but he'll be fine.

Woody raised his hand, and Ben cringed.

Rich shook his head. "Nope, no questions, Woody. Not now.

"Meantime, Coach Raymond and I will run things with Coach Ferg, Coach Bennett, and Coach Moreland, so nothing will change for you. But let's remember how Coach wants us to practice because you practice like you play. I know we've been whipping people's behinds, and we're gonna keep doing that these next couple weeks too. But what Coach would tell you is that these next three weeks of practice are really about Penn Yan and a championship. And that . . . will be a battle."

Raymond nodded in silent agreement. Rich blew his whistle, and practice began. The running and agility work cooled Ben's boiling brain. When his teammates began Oklahoma drills, Ben went to the far end zone to work with Rich as usual. They ran through their quarterback drills without mention of their dad. Ben felt a stab of guilt when he realized that he hadn't even thought about his dad.

During water breaks, Ben kept to himself. When anyone tried to speak to him, he held his head down until they went away. On the final water break, before the team segment of practice, Thea knelt down beside him. She said nothing, but he could see her out of the corner of his eye.

Finally, she placed a hand on his shoulder pad. "I know you don't want to talk about it. I totally get that. But I want you to know that I know he's gonna get better. Your dad's like an ox, and he's a great guy. What he did for me? No one outside my family ever made me feel like I belonged. Please tell him I'm praying for him."

Ben looked up to see her walking away.

After Sunday's win against East Rochester, Ben and his brothers drove straight up the Thruway to the hospital.

"Bo had five touchdown passes, Mom. Five. You should have seen him!" Raymond threw his hands in the air.

Their mom gave them a weak smile and pulled Ben into a hug. "I'm sorry I missed it. You didn't get hit in the head, did you?"

"No, Ma." Ben wiggled free.

"So how is he?" Rich had worn a frown from the moment they left the truck.

Their mom's eyes glistened, but she nodded. "He's okay. His temperature is down to a hundred and he smiled the last time he was up. I think it was a smile, right, Rose?"

Rose appeared tired and sad. She nodded slowly. "I think so."

"Has he moved his legs?" Raymond asked.

"You should go in. Take Ben. You can all go. Rose and I will get some coffee. Anyone want?"

No one did.

"I thought only two people are allowed at a time?" Ben said. His mom had a habit of bending if not breaking the rules.

She dismissed his question with an impatient wave of her hand. "I'm friends with the nurses."

Ben watched them go, then followed his brothers. Their dad lay much the same as the last five times he'd visited. If anything, the pale skin of his face had taken on a faint yellow tint. Rich grabbed some tissues next to the bed and wiped some drool from the corner of their dad's mouth. He groaned and swatted at Rich's hand without opening his eyes.

"That's a good sign," said Rich.

Raymond put both hands on the beds railing. "Dad, Bo threw five touchdown passes."

"He can't hear you. He's out of it." Rich slumped down in a chair and pulled out his phone.

Raymond sat on the window ledge dangling his feet and buried his head in his own phone.

Ben stood beside the bed looking down on his dad. The low whirring of the ventilator kept an alternating rhythm with the steady hissing of his dad's breath. As Ben stood, the hypnotic sounds lulled him into a daze.

He grabbed the cold metal railing and held on.

Ben's mom slept at the hospital every night on one of the chairs that folded out into a narrow bed. Ben stayed in his own house with Jessica and Rich, but sometimes after practice he would stay with Cara and Raymond in their house down the street. In school, all anyone wanted to talk about was the upcoming fall dance.

Ben sat with his teammates at lunch. Woody acted as the main go-between with the girls, carrying notes back and forth and adding dashes of his own wit in commentaries included with each delivery.

"Tuna, Kristina Collins must need glasses, but here you go, big guy."

"Emma Sweeney is the queen of sixth grade and Woody's the king, but she's got her heart set on the court jester. Here you go, Malik."

"All the girls are sweet on Benjamin, but he's simply so sour that there's no need to even ask." Woody held the note high while he shredded it into confetti, then showered it down on Ben's head.

He ignored the laughter, dusted himself off, and finished the last of his bacon chicken ranch sub with one big bite. Ben didn't care one bit about some girl sitting across the cafeteria wanting to go with him to the dance.

He had other plans.

64

The days sped by.

The hillsides surrounding the lake blazed orange. Leaves began to fall, spinning and drifting down on the backs of chilly breezes. Honking geese flew high overhead in scribbled formations across deep blue skies. Pumpkins began to haunt doorsteps with grinning faces promising Halloween.

Ben barely noticed. His days began in darkened mornings with a rush for school. He took his studies more seriously than his friends with the exception of Malik, who wanted to become a doctor like his mom and dad. After school, Rich or Raymond would pick him up and take him to the hospital to see his mom and dad.

His mom's face had grown long. Rosie had returned to Harvard for some midterm exams, leaving his mom alone. His dad seemed frozen in time, and that weighed everyone down.

After the hospital, they'd grab fast food, eating it in the truck on the way home. Ben would change into his football gear at home and off they'd go to practice.

Rich and Raymond more than made up for their dad's absence. When teammates grumbled their complaints to Ben, he'd simply reply, "Penn Yan."

It wasn't until the Thursday before the second-to-last game that Ben could bring himself to hang on to the football Thea just snapped to him. She held out her hands, waiting. Ben stared at her, tongue-tied. They had removed themselves, as they always did before practice began, to the far end zone.

She thrusted her open hands at him a second time. "What?"

He cleared his throat. "The sixth-grade dance here is tomorrow night."

Ben glanced nervously at the rest of the team. They filled the air with chatter, shouts, and laughter muted by the distance between them.

Thea stared at him, waiting for more. "Yeah, so?"

Ben gaped at her pretty face, her delicate upturned nose, and her sparkling blue eyes. "Well, pretty much everyone's going, so . . ."

"Pretty late notice, isn't it?"

Ben continued to stare, wondering now if he might not get sick.

"I mean, did you ask a bunch of girls and no one said yes? Am I the last resort here?"

"What? No! No."

A small smile crept onto her face. "If you want to ask me to the dance, then just ask me, Ben."

Ben wondered why she couldn't just make it easy. He wanted to tell her that he had girls asking *him* to the dance, but somehow he didn't think that would go over so well. "So will you?"

"What? Will I what?" She stamped her foot.

He looked down at the grass and scuffed it up with a cleated foot. "Will you go to the dance with me?"

"Will *I* go to a dance with only one day's notice with *you*? Well, let me think . . . I guess . . . I guess no."

Ben's head snapped up. "Huh?"

She laughed at him and pointed. "Got you! Yeah, I'll go. Thanks for asking, even though I had to drag it out of you."

Raymond blew his whistle. They turned and ran over to join the team. Ben felt funny but excited throughout practice. He avoided Thea during water breaks and caught himself barking out the cadence extra loud. He had no idea why.

After practice, Ben made a beeline for the truck. He had his fingers wrapped around the door handle when he felt tapping on his shoulder pad. He turned and there she stood.

"What time tomorrow night?"

"Oh, uh, seven thirty, and it's over at ten." Ben couldn't keep his eyes from looking over her shoulder for signs of any of his friends.

Thea peeked behind her to see the source of his distraction.

She then gave him a puzzled look. "I'll go home and change after practice; then one of my brothers will probably drive us. We'll pick you up at your house. This isn't anything formal, right?"

"No, no. Your brothers?" Ben's voice cracked.

"Brother. Not brothers. Hopefully David. He's nicer than Kevin, but only by a little."

Ben couldn't imagine what it would be like having one of those beasts driving them to and from the dance. He did a quick calculation of the total time he'd be exposed to one of those brutes—twenty minutes, tops.

That was twenty too many. "Don't they . . . have a game?"

"Nah, they play Liverpool in the Dome Saturday night."

"Well, one of my brothers can take us too."

She held up her hands. "No, my brothers have been talking about this for as long as I can remember."

"Talking about what?" Ben chuckled, expecting some kind of punch line.

Thea tilted her head. "About my first date. I wouldn't be surprised if they both end up taking us. Then you'll see some fireworks. Whew."

"Fireworks between them, right?"

"Yeah, well, you never know with those two, but you'll be fine. Don't look so worried."

Her eager look might as well have been a punch in the gut. "Well, I see my brothers coming. So tomorrow night it is."

66

Ben was nervous the whole next day. He had no stomach for lunch.

He got Mr. Sofia to give him a library pass. He checked out the sports section of the online newspaper on one of the computers and instantly regretted it when the front page featured an article complete with a quarter-page photo of the mighty Labourdette twins. "Mean and Nasty" headlined the story.

Just as Thea said, David was mean, but Kevin was downright nasty. David relentlessly rushed the passer. He ran by blockers or through them. He led the entire state with twenty-one quarterback sacks in the previous season. No one in the state boasted more tackles to date this season than Kevin, with 159. Kevin also led the league in violent penalties—roughing the passer, unsportsmanlike conduct, and unnecessary roughness—thus the "Nasty" moniker.

"Hey, buddy."

Ben jumped in his seat. He turned to see Tuna, who clapped a paw onto his shoulder.

Ben quickly minimized the window on his screen.

"Hey, yeah. Thea's brothers, man, bad dudes. I read that article at breakfast. Eleven unnecessary roughness penalties for Nasty. That's more than one a game." Tuna slowly wagged his big head. "My sister is friends with a guy on their team, and he told her that they're even worse in practice, fighting all the time. He said everyone poops their pants around them, even the *coaches*."

Ben selected another story and filled the screen with girls' soccer box scores.

Tuna gazed at him like a pirate sizing up his loot. "What are you doing in here, man?"

"I felt kinda queasy, so I didn't want to eat and I got S to give me a pass." Ben didn't like being grilled, but he didn't want to create more suspicion by dodging Tuna's questions.

Tuna nodded slowly. "Well, we missed you. Seems like everyone's got a date for tonight but you. Even Finn got reeled in by Sara Camy. You're planning on going, right?"

"I, uh, really don't know. I gotta see how I feel. I might have to go visit my dad." It was true. Ben wasn't sure he really wanted to ride to and from the dance with two maniacs watching his every move and passing judgment on his every word. He had the perfect excuse to bail.

Tuna's face turned sober. "Yeah. Of course. Any change?"

"No. He's still out of it." Ben looked away, out the window.

"Your dad's a rhinoceros, Ben. He's gonna pull through,

no doubt." Tuna's face said he truly believed, but Tuna was no doctor, and he seemed to be forgetting that it was more than just pneumonia. ALS changed the game.

"Thanks, buddy." Over Tuna's shoulder Ben spied Mrs. Feltz heading straight for them like an angry wasp.

"Yeah, and I'm sorry. It's just a stupid dance. I bet tonight's the night he snaps out of it." Tuna's voice had the upbeat sound of a coach at halftime.

"*Mr.* Tonelli, evidently you just marched yourself right here without a pass, and unless you show me a pass this instant, you'll be spending your afternoon with Mr. Seevy." Mrs. Feltz had a cranky heart and a voice to go with it. She thrust her hand in Tuna's face. "Your pass, Anthony."

"Mrs. Feltz, how many times have I told you? I'm Tuna, Big Tuna to those who don't know me. I also answer to Mr. Big if you prefer a more formal name. The Tuna doesn't believe in passes, Mrs. Feltz, as both you and Mr. Seevy already know. The Tuna believes he has constitutional rights that allow him to travel between the states and the classrooms with the freedom our forefathers fought and died for."

"That's enough, Mr. Tonelli. Come with me."

Tuna grinned and walked behind Mrs. Feltz without a word.

He paused and turned to look back at Ben. "Yeah, I bet you tonight's the night he pulls through, Ben. I can feel it."

Ben forced a smile and said to himself, "We'll see."

Ben waged a war against himself over what to do.

After school Raymond picked him up, Fridays being light days at his work.

"What's wrong, Bo?" Ben had barely taken his seat, but Raymond wasn't a mental health counselor by accident. He had a knack for being able to read people the way a Boy Scout reads a map.

"Nothing."

"Yeah? Okay." That's what Raymond did. He'd just sit and outwait you until you broke. One time Ben heard Raymond tell their dad that he waited five weeks for a teenage girl client to talk.

Two-thirds of the way to the hospital, Ben decided that the teenage girl must have had some kind of superpowers.

He gave up with a sigh. "So there's this dance tonight."

"Uh-huh." Raymond didn't even take his eyes off the road.

"And, well, I asked Thea, but now . . . I don't know, Raymond. She wants one of her brothers to drive us, maybe both."

"And they're beasts." Raymond unsuccessfully fought back a smile.

"Why is that funny?"

Raymond glanced at him. "It's not. You're growing up, Brother. Your first date. I'm happy for you. She's some girl. Pretty too."

"Did you even hear what I said?" Ben slapped the dashboard.

"Are her brothers really the reason, or do you think it could be something else?" Raymond's voice only softened.

Ben felt steam building in his brain. "Of course it's her brothers. What else could it be?"

"You tell me," Raymond practically whispered.

"Is this really what you do for a living? Because you're annoying the snot out of me."

Silence. Ben wanted to scream.

They pulled into the hospital entrance. Raymond rounded the circle and turned into the parking garage. He found a spot, turned off the engine, and just sat there saying nothing.

"Are we going, or what?" Ben threw his hands in the air.

"Your call."

Ben felt the steam jetting out his ears. Then it cleared. "I don't know if it's a good thing to take my own center to a dance."

"Yeah, that's the real problem, right? What's Tuna and Woody and Rohan going to say?"

"We got Penn Yan next week. We don't need any extra drama." Ben looked over to find Raymond studying him.

"So you regret asking her?"

"I regret it and I don't. Does that even make sense?" Ben searched his brother's eyes.

"Perfect sense. Now you have a choice, take some flak from your buddies, or humiliate a key player going into the championship game."

"Humiliate? How?"

Raymond shrugged. "I'm sure she told her friends, her parents, the brothers."

"But I can say I had to visit Dad. She can't feel bad then, right?"

Raymond shook his head. "What happens when you lie? Don't you usually have to lie again, and again, and again?"

Ben had to nod. That's usually the way things went, and then you ended up in an even bigger mess.

"Remember when Rich played his senior season and he was the big star quarterback, setting records, undefeated season and all that?"

"Yeah." Ben was only in second grade at the time, but he sure remembered that.

"So there was this kid everyone made fun of, Alex Slank. Alex had a colostomy, no large intestine, so he had this bag on his hip that carried his waste. It would smell sometimes, so people called him 'Stank,' rhymes with Slank, right? Not Rich, though. He called him Alex, and he had him sit with the football players at lunch. He wouldn't let anyone call Alex anything but Alex.

"Pretty soon, the whole team started to take pride in protecting Alex. If anyone called him names or picked on him and one of the football players heard it? That kid got to slow dance with the lockers. Bam! Face-first."

"That's a great story, but I'm talking about a dance."

"The point is that Rich is a leader. He doesn't care what people say about him. He's far from perfect, but Rich? If his team ever got down? He'd keep his head high and keep going like he believed that nothing could stop them, and nothing could.

"You may end up in that situation at Penn Yan. You know, Ben, if Mom gets her way—and she usually does—this might be it, your last game. If it is, this game will be the one you remember for the rest of your life, win or lose." Raymond reached for the door handle.

"Wait," Ben said. "You're telling me to beat Penn Yan, I gotta take Thea to some crummy dance?"

Raymond laughed. "All I'm saying is that people judge you by your actions. That's it. Now let's get in there. Maybe Dad's gonna finally be awake."

68

"No change." Ben's mom stared up at them from a chair beside their dad's bed with hollow eyes and a hollow voice.

He lay in the bed, mouth open with a glinting stream of spittle running down his cheek and losing itself in the tangle of a sheet and a flimsy yellow hospital blanket. The serpent of ribbed tubing hissed while the face of a monitor smiled its jagged smile and winked its red demon eyes. The beeping of an IV medicine dispenser ricocheted off the walls before piercing Ben's boiled brain.

Their mom seemed not to notice.

"What can we do?" Raymond gently rubbed their mom's shoulder.

She turned her head toward their dad. "Just wait. Maybe pray. I don't know. That's what he'd say."

"No, Mom. I meant for *you*, what can I—we—what can we do for you?"

"Oh, I'm fine. I just wish . . . I just wish . . ." When she looked back at them, tears filled her eyes, but she sniffed them back and frowned. "I curse that game."

"Mom, Dad loves it. He doesn't blame football." Raymond pulled a tissue from a box on the window ledge and handed it to her.

"Don't even get me started, Raymond." A tiger couldn't have given a more ferocious look.

Raymond only pursed his lips and slowly nodded. "How about some coffee? We'll go with you. Bo and I can get one of those grilled Cuban sandwiches. We gotta eat before practice anyway."

"I can't leave him alone."

Ben stepped forward. "I'll stay. You guys go and bring me back a Cuban and some curly fries. Lots of ketchup."

Ben saw the doubt on her face. "I'll talk to him, Mom."

Her eyes sparked. "Dr. Cohen said it's good to talk to him. You could tell him about the bald eagle you all saw last weekend, and what your plans are for Halloween. Remember the pumpkins he used to carve for you kids?"

"I know what to say." Ben helped her up out of the chair.

"You're sure, Benjamin?"

Raymond gave a thumbs-up behind her back, so Ben shooed her away. "Yes. I'm sure. Lots of ketchup."

Raymond placed a hand on her back and gently moved her toward the door. They disappeared around the corner. Ben heard them talking about Cara's job until the sounds of the hospital swallowed their voices. He peeked out into the hall and looked around before softly closing the door. He sat in his mom's chair for a minute, studying the stream from the corner of his dad's mouth.

He stood and grabbed a couple tissues, then mopped up the drool all the way down his dad's neck. A large oval wet spot blemished the pillow. Ben grabbed three more tissues and slipped them under his dad's neck.

He stood back and looked around. "Hi, Dad."

He felt ridiculous. What if a nurse walked in? But when his mom returned, she would without a doubt grill him on the content of his one-way conversation. He thought of telling her a story, but that was just a fancy term for a lie. With Raymond's opinion about lies so fresh in his mind, he knew that he couldn't bring himself to do that.

He sat back down, but only for a minute. He stood and wrapped his fingers around the top bar of the bed's railing. "So I invited Thea to this dance. But . . . I guess I got cold feet. I have a feeling I'm gonna get all kinds of razzing from the guys if I show up with her. I don't know what I was thinking. No, that's not true. I like her. . . . Raymond says basically that I should take her and be a leader, and I'm running out of time. . . .

"Dad?"

His dad's eyes fluttered wildly under their lids. His body twitched. Convulsions? The machine staring down lost its smile. Flatline. Red lights flashed, and the alarm buzzed with deafening intensity, like a giant yellow jacket from a nightmare.

"Dad?" The voice couldn't be his, not from so far away, not so overrun with panic?

Nurses and doctors flooded the room sweeping Ben aside.

"Dad!"

Ben stood in the corner, numb and invisible.

His heart was frozen with terror. Ben had a horrible nagging feeling that he should do something, to help in some way. He thought of his mom, watching, day after day, hour by hour, but now absent at the end. Maybe that was for the best.

"I've got a pulse!" a nurse yelled. They were the most beautiful words Ben had ever heard.

Hope rushed in.

His dad twisted back and forth, struggling against the hands holding him down. Ben stepped forward and peered at his dad's face. His opened eyes flashed with anger, then settled on Ben and softened.

"Dad, it's okay." Ben fought back the tears filling his eyes.

His dad settled back into the bed, his eyes locked on Ben. Ben stepped closer and took his dad's hand in both of his.

The fingers moved, but barely.

The doctor, a pretty young woman, bent over Ben's dad and spoke to him as if he were a child. "Mr. Redd, you've been asleep for almost two weeks. You're doing well, but I need you to just relax and not pull at your IV or the wires connected to your monitors. Okay?"

His dad nodded, but he gently touched the hissing tube with a question in his eyes for the doctor.

"That's your trach tube." She still spoke as though to a child, and Ben wished she'd stop. "You had pneumonia and we needed to give you a tracheotomy to help you breathe, but you're doing well now, really well. I need you to relax, though, and not pull at these wires or your IV or your trach. Okay? Good."

Ben quickly texted his mom and Raymond. He continued to stand by the bed, holding his dad's hand and babbling on about their last two games and how Raymond and Rich did a great job, but it wasn't the same without him.

When Raymond and their mom returned, she kissed their dad's face all over without saying a word.

Ben quickly ate, finishing his sandwich as Raymond looked at his phone. "Okay, Bo. We gotta move."

They kissed their mom and dad and said they'd be back tomorrow.

On the ride home, they talked about nothing but their dad. Ben changed quickly into his uniform, and they arrived at practice just in time for stretching. Rich made a show of looking at his watch but then seemed to read the expression on Raymond's face. Ben hopped into a line and grinned at the sight of his brothers hugging.

In his joy, Ben had forgotten all about the dance until their first water break when he felt a tap on the back of his shoulder pads. He turned around.

Thea had a dirt-smudged face and French braids in her hair that looked like rows of corn. She looked more like a UFC fighter than a date.

Her mouthpiece warped her smile and garbled her speech. "So ow abow seven thirty?"

70

Ben could only smile stupidly and nod like a clown. "Yeah. Great."

She gave him a funny look, half-puzzled, half-annoyed. "We don't have to do this, you know."

Freedom suddenly reared its head. She said it, not him. Only nine days remained in their season. After that, would he ever even see her again? Certainly not if he bailed on her tonight.

Instead, Ben said, "Why would you say that?"

"I don't know. You don't seem all that excited," she said.

"My dad woke up today."

"Well, if you want to see him, I totally understand."

By making it so easy, she caused him to doubt himself, and maybe feel a little jealous of some unknown alternate who had asked her as well. Ben studied his other teammates as they joked and smiled and drank. He racked his brain to remember who had dates and who didn't. He wished he'd paid closer attention. Could it be Rohan? Finn? Malik? Certainly not Tuna or Woody. But why not?

"No. I'm good if you are."

She smiled around her mouthpiece. "Okay, pick you up at seven thirty."

The purple pickup pulled to a stop in front of the house.

It rumbled and shook, puking diesel smoke from two tall chrome exhaust pipes fixed to the hind quarters of the cab. Jessica had helped Ben dress in black driving shoes and gray pants with a matching black Under Armour golf shirt. The truck door opened, and Thea scooted over into the middle seat, snuggling against Mean or Nasty. Ben had no way of knowing one twin from the other.

He jumped in and buckled up. "Hi, Thea."

"Hi, Ben." She beamed, sunshine and rainbows. "This is my brother Kevin."

So Nasty it was.

Ben extended a hand across Thea. "Nice to meet you, Na—Kevin."

Nasty glanced down at Ben's hand before revving the

engine and slamming the truck into gear. After being thrown into the back of his seat, Ben remained quiet, even though the silent ride begged for some small talk.

They pulled into the school's drop-off circle near the gymnasium entrance and stopped behind Tuna's mom in her big Mercedes sedan. She had her phone to her ear, and Tuna and his date were nowhere to be seen. The circle had emptied out in front of her, and Nasty Kevin leaned on his horn. Tuna's mom ignored them. Kevin raced the engine and violently swerved around her blaring the horn all the while.

"You fool!" Kevin shouted.

They lurched to a stop, and Ben scrambled out of the truck. It took all his willpower to turn and calmly help Thea down.

Kevin looked at them the way Ben imagined he looked at opposing running backs. "Nine thirty. Don't make me wait."

Thea slammed the door shut, and the big purple truck took off, leaving them in a cloud of rancid-smelling diesel.

"Sorry about that. He's getting his mind ready for the Liverpool game."

Ben looked at her, really for the first time, under the white lamp light. She took his breath away and he tried not to gawk, but she was beautiful. A mane of blonde hair framed her face and spilled down and around the shoulders of the black cotton dress that fell to the top of her knees. Her perfectly formed legs ended with dainty feet in a pair of black strappy sandals.

Her slightly upturned nose gave her an elfin quality. Her blue eyes sparkled like rare gems, and the hint of pink lipstick left his face warm.

"That's . . . I get it. My brothers were the same way. Wow,

you really look great. Hey, you're shivering. I'm sorry. Let's get inside." Ben held his open hand down by her hip, and an electric current surged through his body when she took it in her own.

Ben blushed as he gave two tickets to Mr. Sofia, who sat at his table and offered up a bashful smile of his own.

Music from the gym pounded through the halls. As they neared the open doors, they saw the flashing, spinning lights.

"Oh, I love this song. C'mon, let's dance." Her grip tightened on his hand.

In they went.

Rich and Ben woke early and headed over to the hospital the next day. Ben relayed the details of the dance to Rich on the drive over. "It was a fun night."

"So it all worked out with Thea, huh. Did any of the guys say anything about it?"

"Nah," Ben replied. But Tuna did give him a look when he walked in with Thea on his arm.

Rich pulled up to the hospital and parked. As they entered their dad's room, he was wildly waving his arms about while wearing a look of utter frustration. The alphabet was printed on a small board covering his lap. His dad was pointing to letters to communicate, since he wasn't able to talk. The doctor held a notebook-sized board with the words GAME, COACH, CHAMPIONSHIP.

The doctor smiled warmly while shaking her head. "I'm

sorry, I understand what you're trying to say. You have the championship game on Sunday, but Monday is the absolute earliest we can discharge you, and even that is really stretching it, Mr. Redd."

Ben's mom patted the doctor's arm. "Believe me. He's like this at home too. Always pushing, but that's what got him where he is."

Rich and Ben headed over to practice after staying another thirty minutes. Rich reported to the team that Coach wouldn't be out of the hospital for Sunday's game, but that a win would be the best get-well present he could get. "So let's be sharp, tonight and in tomorrow's walk-through, and bring home a championship."

They practiced hard. On the drive home, Rich looked over at Ben when they had stopped at a traffic light. "What's the matter, Bo? You look like you had some bad sushi."

He shrugged without meeting Rich's eye. "I'm okay."

"Is it Dad? He's gonna be fine. Look how far he's come." Rich returned his attention to the road as the light turned green. "And he'll be home soon."

"But not in time for the game. You think we can win without him?" Ben stole a glance at his brother long enough to see his face redden.

"Why? You think we can't?" Rich laughed bitterly. "I've run this offense for a lot of years. Dad's a defensive guy, but Raymond knows what he's doing. You better get your head right, Bo. This is probably gonna be the last football game you ever play, and you don't want to mess yourself."

"Last game? Who says?"

Rich gave him a superior smile. "Mom. You know that."

"Dad says I can. Raymond thinks so too."

Rich shook his head and laughed. "Okay, you know more than me."

Ben scowled at his brother, but Rich turned on the radio.

Ben raised his voice above the music. "You know the offense, but Dad came up with the fake reverse in the middle of the Geneva game last year. Same thing with the 92 defense in the middle of the Marcus Whitman game. We need Dad. When he says something, everyone believes it."

They both knew the game swam through their dad's veins. He knew what to do when things went wrong. He could decode an opponent and design a play or an adjustment that would work like magic.

Rich snorted, but he could do little more than that because he knew Ben spoke the truth.

Rich stayed quiet only once in a blue moon, so Ben kept going. "And Penn Yan? They're gonna be bigger than us, meaner than us, stronger than us, and faster than us. That's just the way it is. So yeah. It's hard to get all pumped up when I know we need Dad and he's gonna be sitting in his hospital bed."

"Yeah, he's our El Cid, no doubt." Rich sounded almost repentant.

"El Cid?"

"El Cid was a famous Spanish warlord. I did a report on him my junior year in high school. When he died during a siege, his wife had his body dressed up in his armor and put onto his horse to ride into battle, striking fear into the hearts of the enemy and raising the spirits of his men to win the battle."

"Dad's not dead, Rich." Even the notion disturbed Ben.

Rich shook his head, smiling, but not as broadly as before. "I'm just agreeing with you. He's our leader. Just to have him on the sideline is a big deal to the team, but we have to find a way to win without him. A big part of that is you. Kids look up to you. You're the leader out there, Bo. So you *gotta* believe."

Ben nodded like he knew that already and he was fine.

In truth, it made his stomach somersault.

73

Sunday, the weatherman called for rain all day with a high of fifty-three degrees, just cold enough with the wet and the wind to make things miserable for a spread offense. The gray sky's belly hung low, drizzling rain. Puddles, swamps, and streams exhaled a mild fog, and the wipers worked steadily to clear the windshield.

"This stinks." Ben didn't need any more adversity to insure a barfing incident on the sideline.

"Football, Bo. Part of the game." Raymond squinted through the glass as a tractor trailer whooshed past, creating its own private hurricane.

"Remind me to go to school someplace like Texas. Better yet, Miami. That's a decent school, right?" Ben shivered and crossed his arms.

"You keep playing how you're playing and you keep working

hard, you'll go wherever you want." Raymond reached down and turned on the heat.

They rode for a while with cars and trucks swishing past.

Ben warmed his hands, rubbing them briskly under a vent. "Rich said this is my last game."

"Is it?" Raymond looked alarmed.

"He said Mom isn't letting me play after this, but Dad told me I could."

Raymond glanced his way. "Then I'd say you can. Mom gets her way most of the time, but when Dad digs in? You don't want to be around."

Ben thought about that for a moment. "Sounds like my call."

"I'd say."

"You think Rich is right? All that stuff about even high school football players getting, you know, the thing that Chris Gedney had?" Ben studied his brother's face.

"CTE?" Raymond pursed his lips. "If it's true, a lot of people are in trouble, including him and me."

"And Dad."

"We got a lot of time to think about all that. Let's focus on today. Let's get this win. It's not gonna be your last game if you don't want it to be, but it is the last time the four brothers are gonna be on the same team. Next year you'll be on the middle school team."

Four brothers was what the three of them and their dad called themselves whenever they all did something together— trips to Atlanta to watch the Falcons play, or a hike, or a boat ride, or watching the Saturday-night fights. Ben's football team had to be the biggest thing the four brothers had ever done together. Raymond's mention of the four brothers didn't make Ben feel any better. It only highlighted the brokenness of the dreary day.

He stared out the window at the soggy farm fields. The trees stood almost naked now, with only scraps of dying brown leaves to remind him of the beauty that was. The day matched his mood.

Like Skaneateles, Penn Yan rested at the northern tip of a Finger Lake named Keuka. On a map, Keuka Lake looked like a wishbone. Three more Finger Lakes stood between the two, and the drive took over an hour. Maybe it was the stress, or a bad night's sleep, or the heat washing over him, but whatever the cause, Ben dozed off.

After a time, he jumped awake. Raymond smiled over at him as he wiped some drool from the corner of his mouth. He sat up straight and stared. Outside, patches of blue shone through random tears in the clouds. A band of golden light beamed down through one such opening, bringing a distant tree-covered hillside to life. A grove of sturdy oaks held strong to its leaves and glowed like an orange gemstone.

By the time they pulled into the stadium, the sun dominated a blue sky with scattered clouds like great, puffy blimps cruising to the east. The stadium had been built into a hillside. The home team's stands dwarfed the visitors single set of bleachers. Already half the town's families dressed in Penn Yan orange and royal blue filled the seats. The third- and fourth-grade teams were wrapping up their game, a 48–6 blowout that put the home team fans in a festive mood to match the smells of hot dogs and cotton candy, and the sights of blue and orange balloons and face paint.

Penn Yan loved its football.

Ben got down from his brother's truck and took a deep breath, feeling a bit like Colonel Custer, hopelessly surrounded by his enemy. Half the team had already gathered on a grassy plateau across from the main entrance to the high school that crowned the hilltop. They warmed up without the usual confident chatter of prior Sunday mornings. Ben felt robotic and sensed an undercurrent of dread despite the upbeat cheerleading by his brothers. Tuna's eyes bugged out of his head. Woody was quiet as a lamb. Even Malik, the standard of excellence, messed up the simplest assignments.

Before he knew it, he found himself stamping down the paved road on their way to the stadium. They marched in two lines with Ben and Thea in the lead.

"What's wrong with everyone?" Thea spoke in an undertone only Ben could hear. "Are they *scared*?"

Ben cringed because he had to ask himself that very question. Was he?

No. Not scared, but sickened. Was there a difference? He surely couldn't ask Thea for fear she'd lose all respect for him.

"Why do you say that?" he asked in the same quiet voice.

She glanced back. "Everyone's so stiff. Look at Tuna's eyes. He looks like a lemur. Rohan keeps tying and untying his cleats, and I caught Finn talking to himself."

"It's a big game. The championship. Perfect season on the line." Ben felt almost proud of the words that came out of his mouth.

"When Kevin and Dave played for the state championship last year, they had to practically be restrained by their coach before the game. He had to take them out of the team drill in warm-ups because he was afraid they'd hurt someone."

Ben didn't want to insult her brothers, so he offered no comment, but only gave a knowing nod.

"I mean, you're always quiet before games. That's your thing. You're a quarterback, so it's not like you're bugging out like the rest of these guys." She glanced back again and shook her head in pity. "You know who we need, don't you?"

Before he could even process the question, she said, "Your dad."

Even with a stiff breeze, the broad swatches of sunlight warmed the field to a level nearly perfect for a game of football. Ben had an arm that neutralized the wind, while the Penn Yan quarterback accuracy suffered when he threw into it. From what Ben could see from the Penn Yan warm-ups, that might be the only advantage Skaneateles could expect.

On the sideline after introductions, Tuna grabbed Ben's arm and pointed toward the group of opposing players gathered in the end zone for introductions of their own. "See that kid?"

"What kid?" Ben yanked his arm free from Tuna's vise grip.

Tuna snorted. "C'mon, you see him. You can't miss him. *That* kid!"

Now he saw. The boy, if he was a boy and not a man, stood an inch or two over six feet. He towered over his teammates, and they had more than a handful of linemen built like ogres.

"Oh. Yeah. I see *him*."

"You think he's right D end, or left? He could be left to stop the run. You know most people in this league run the ball, and even though we're a passing team, if he played left all season, they might not want to switch him, right? What do *you* think?" Tuna's eyes bugged out even more than before. His voice quavered.

"Relax, buddy. You can handle him. You're the Big Tuna." Ben grabbed him by the upper arms and gave him a shake.

Tuna looked like he might cry. "So you think left. Blind side. I knew it."

"I don't know anything. I'm just saying if he's across from you, you can handle him. C'mon, big guy. You handled that kid from JE."

"This guy makes that guy look like a popcorn fart."

"Tuna, you gotta stop. Believe in yourself, man. *I* do! 'Star-Spangled Banner.' Let's go." Ben dragged him along to the sideline to stand tall for the anthem.

Ben left his friend for the coin toss.

Tuna's nightmare and two ogres captained Penn Yan. The Nightmare towered over the ref and wore a blank stare worse than any twisted snarl. Ben cringed at the sight of Thea sandwiched between him and Malik. He remembered the moment of her holding his hand as they entered the gymnasium for the dance, and she turned everyone's head. That seemed like a dream looking at her now, snarling up at her foes, fearless, almost rabid.

The Nightmare looked at her with mild curiosity. The ogres grinned and jostled each other over their private joke. Thea sneered.

Malik called heads, and they won the toss. Rich had insisted that they defer so they'd get the ball after halftime, so Penn Yan took the ball, but Ben had the wind. They all shook hands—the ogres laughing out loud now—and returned to their sidelines.

Rich stood in the center of the team. "All right, defense is up. They're big, but we're tough. Bring it in! Malik, you break 'em down."

"Huh, huh, huh, huh, huh . . ."

"Break it down!"

The cheers, howls, and growls lacked real heart. Ben cringed and looked at his brothers, who pretended not to notice.

"Okay, kickoff team, then D, you're up!" Raymond shouted while clapping his hands. "Bring it in here, D! Listen, I want you all to run to the ball, hear me? No matter where it is, we run to the ball until you hear the whistle. Just like we did in practice. All right, let's go!"

The kickoff team kept Penn Yan inside their own forty, not great, but not bad. The defense took the field. The Nightmare wore number seventeen, and he lined up at wide receiver. Ben stood with his toes on the line and put his hands on his knees to watch.

The quarterback took the snap and tossed the ball to the running back sprinting toward Ben's sideline, a power sweep. Everyone ran for the ball. Ben smelled a rat. Number 17 blocked the cornerback in front of him, but it didn't feel real. It wasn't. Number 17 peeled back toward the running back.

Ben shouted at the top of his lungs. "Reverse! Reverse! Reverse!"

Too little, too late.

Number 17 ran like the wind, against the grain, down the opposite sideline, and into the end zone. Penn Yan tried a short pass into the end zone for the extra points, but Thea broke up the pass. Twenty-three seconds into the game, Ben's team trailed by six. Whatever half-hearted enthusiasm Ben's team-mates had gone out the window.

Penn Yan lined up for the kickoff.

Rich screamed encouragement from the sideline, then gathered his offensive troops. "All right, guys, this game might be a shoot-out, so we're going to air it out while we've got the wind to our backs."

Suddenly, the Penn Yan crowd went wild. Rich spun around, and all eyes darted to the field, where a Penn Yan player dodged through the Skaneateles return team and danced into the end zone. Their offense ran in the extra points straight up the gut behind the two ogres who plowed the defenders aside like bowling pins to take a 14–0 lead. Less than a minute had run off the clock.

Rich grabbed Raymond. "What happened?"

"They pooch kicked it to Harding. He caught it and froze. They just ripped it right out of his hands." Raymond's voice reeked of this defeat.

In his bones, Ben knew he needed to lead his team to a score on the next series, or they could kiss their championship goodbye.

75

This time, Penn Yan ran an on-side kick.

The refs peeled players off a haystack of bodies while the whole stadium held its breath. Raymond squeezed his own head between his hands. Rich looked up at the sky, cursing to himself. When Rohan popped up holding the ball, Ben sighed with relief. The Skaneateles bleachers floated up a lackluster cheer for the minor victory.

The first play Rich called hitch and go, a deep pass. Ben saw Number 17 lined up across from Tuna. Since the play went to Finn, Ben would be looking to what would normally be his blind side. If Tuna didn't hold his block for very long, at least Ben could avoid a brutal hit in the back. In that moment, Ben realized that he hadn't thrown up before the game. He smiled to himself thinking that it must be an omen.

He looked right to give Damon a fake nod, then left to give

Finn the real one. He called the cadence and took the snap. He faked the hitch to Finn. The cornerback bit. In that same instant, Number 17 faked an inside rush, clubbed Tuna to send him crashing into Jake, then slipped back to the outside with a free run at Ben.

Ben sensed Finn streaking past the cornerback, but he needed to do something about the Nightmare first. He dipped right, then cut left to the wide-open space that Finn had vacated. Number 17 went by him like a bullet, but half a step later, Ben felt like he'd jumped onto a carnival ride. Number 17 had reached out with his giant wingspan, grabbed a handful of Ben's sleeve, and whipped him into the air.

Backward and around he went, up in the air, and then crashing down. The turf came at him like a punch. Ben saw stars on impact. His brain went fuzzy and he gasped for air, a fish on the dock, or an ALS patient in a hospital bed.

Somehow, he'd hung on to the ball.

Tuna and Thea helped him to his feet, then steadied him as he staggered a few steps back.

"You okay?" Thea spoke softly in his ear.

Tuna spoke in a voice that could be heard in the last row of seats. "Dude, he put a move on me like I've never seen. Guy's a freak. He's going to the NFL, dude, no doubt. No one can block that guy. Tell Richie we gotta roll the other way, and even then, you gotta watch your back."

Thea grabbed him by the face mask. "You cream puff! Toughen up! Block your guy!"

Tuna gasped at the insult. "You . . . You're a girl!"

"Well, that's a brilliant discovery!" Thea walked away and took up her position at center.

Tuna, outraged, glared at Ben, who shrugged. "Line up. Let's go, Tuna."

Rich did exactly what Tuna had in mind. Ben rolled out right the next play. He watched the patterns bloom like flowers and the defenders chasing like bees. In that same instant, his sixth sense flashed red. The danger from behind hurried his throw, but all those summer days in the yard with Rich paid off. The release sent the ball spinning in a perfect spiral with the exact trajectory to hit Damon on a corner route.

The hit from behind whipped him face-first into the turf.

More stars.

More pain.

Ben peeled himself off the turf. Number 17 grinned at him, then turned to celebrate, a violent group hug with the ogres. The play netted twenty-two yards and a first down, but Penn Yan's D line considered the punishment to Ben a victory despite the gain. Ben stood tall, though, and jogged downfield for the next play, wincing only to himself. He couldn't even look at Tuna.

On the sideline, Rich screamed at the ref. "That's a flag! That's a late hit all day! Are you *blind*?!"

Raymond had a hold of Rich's left arm with his other arm wrapped around Rich's chest to keep him from racing out onto the field.

Ben rolled his hand in the air signaling for Rich to send the play. The ref placed the ball, setting the play clock in motion. Rich finally calmed down enough to have Mr. Moreland signal the freeze play. Ben chuckled to himself. He barked out the cadence, and the entire defense jumped.

When Rich called the same play again, Ben thought it unwise, but it worked, giving Skaneateles another first down.

The Penn Yan coaches went wild, screaming at their players to watch the ball. Ben knew that an instant of hesitation would do a lot to help his O line secure their blocks.

To further slow down the pass rush, Rich ran a handful of bubble screens with some running plays mixed in. Unfortunately, those plays enjoyed little success. Ultimately, they needed Ben's passing to keep the drive alive and put it in the end zone with a rollout pass that left him under a pile of defenders. They missed on the conversation, but scoring a touchdown gave a spark of hope.

Penn Yan's offense began a ground and pound campaign, chewing up yards and clock. Every time they attempted to mix in a pass, Thea jumped it, knocking the pass to the turf. Regardless, Skaneateles trailed 26–6 halfway through the second quarter. Just before halftime on a fourth and sixteen for a penalty-plagued Penn Yan, Thea picked off a post route in the end zone. Ben charged the field with a fist raised over his head until he joined the mob surrounding Thea.

In an attempt to score before halftime, with just fifty-three seconds left on the clock, Rich went to the air. Down the field they went, with Ben taking a pounding. With four seconds left and just thirteen yards from the end zone, Rich called a reverse. Ben took the snap and sprinted for the sideline. Damon faked his block and twisted back around taking a clean handoff and racing into the wave of pursuit. Ben carried out his fake to the five-yard line before peeking over at Damon.

Standing helpless, he watched Damon get knocked out of bounds at the one-yard line before he took a blind-side hit that sent him flying through the air and . . .

Lights-out.

Ben opened his eyes to see Raymond's face hovering in the cloudy blue sky, Rich's too. He tried to sit up, but they held him back.

"Let go!" Ben struggled against them.

"Easy, killer." Raymond eased him up. "You were out."

Panic gripped Ben by the throat. "No. I wasn't. I had my eyes closed. I got hit hard, but I'm good."

"I think you got a concussion, Bo." Rich turned to Raymond. "We can't let him go back in, Raymond."

"Let's slow down, Brother." Raymond looked at Rich. "Let's get him in the end zone, get him some water, and check him out. Then we'll decide."

Rich snorted and shook his head, then threw his hands in the air as he stomped away. Raymond helped Ben to his feet. The rest of the team milled around a bucket of orange slices before plunking themselves down in a ragged half circle around the goal posts. Tuna sat up against a post with his back to the rest of the team.

Raymond hung on to the back of Ben's shoulder pads just below his neck. When Raymond stopped suddenly, he nearly yanked Ben off his feet. Ben looked back at Raymond, then followed his sight line.

What he saw buckled his knees.

77

Their dad sat in a wheelchair.

The same ribbed hose snaked between the hole in his throat and a portable ventilator, now strapped to the back of the chair. He operated the chair with a joystick on the armrest. Their mom followed close behind as he zipped across the turf heading straight for the team. He got there before they did. The team stared like sheep.

"Dad!" Ben rushed to his side and kissed him. His dad reached up and held Ben's head tightly to his own. Ben stepped aside to give his brothers a turn.

Ben turned to hug their mom, then stepped back. "But how?"

His brothers' faces asked the same question.

"You know your father. He hounded them. He nagged them and badgered them nonstop until, I swear, they wanted him gone more than he did." Their mom's eyes sparkled mischievously.

Their dad meanwhile began to hammer his fist on the armrest to his chair.

"Oh, he's at it again," his mom said. "Me this time! Here, here's your dumb board." From against her leg, she raised a small coach's whiteboard and pretended to bop him on the head.

Their dad laughed silently and placed the board on his lap before zipping away, knowing his boys would follow. The other coaches, Bennett, Moreland, Scotty, and Fergy, all greeted him with surprise and warmth. Then their dad motioned impatiently with his head, pointing to the all-caps word at the top of the board.

ADJUSTMENTS
D

He pointed at Raymond and waved him over.

"Wait, have you been here from the beginning?" Raymond asked.

Their dad shook his head, then tapped the board impatiently with the bottom of his marker. Once he had everyone's attention, he pointed to a question he'd written out.

Thea, QBs eyes telling you where pass will go??

Wide-eyed, Thea nodded her head. "Yes, sir."

Ben's dad nodded back, then pointed to a section of the

board titled "Defense 101." Ten men on the line of scrimmage. Cornerbacks, bumping and blitzing with contain. Everyone else in a gap or on the edge racing upfield. That left a single player in the secondary, Thea.

Raymond gaped at the board, then looked their dad in the eye. "You know this is absurd?"

Ben winced. Even though their dad sat in a wheelchair, Ben expected some kind of fireworks. His dad's face remained calm, though. He even nodded to Rich and offered up a smile.

"I love it," said Raymond. "Thea, why didn't you tell me that?"

She shrugged so hard her French braids bounced. "I just figured everyone saw it. That kid looks before the play even begins, and he doesn't stop looking."

Ben's dad laughed silently again and slapped his knee. He cut his smile short, though, and awkwardly flipped the board for offensive adjustments, pointing his marker now at Rich.

Their dad had drawn up Xs and Os of a spread offense and Penn Yan's defense. Instead of an X at the left defensive end position, their dad had substituted Number 17. He pointed to Jake Moreland, then looked around until he spied Tuna pouting. He cast a brief angry glare at Rich and stabbed a finger toward Tuna's back.

Rich's face boiled. "Tuna! Get your butt over here with your team! We're gonna win this thing, and if you want a trophy, you better fly straight!"

Tuna heaved himself up and plopped down next to Ben as if to remind the coaches that he had friends in high places.

Their dad pointed his marker at Jake and Tuna, then

jabbed the circles representing them on the board. He gave one final look at Rich to emphasize the importance of what he was about to show them all. He then drew two arrows to show Tuna and Jake blocking down to the inside leaving Number 17 unblocked.

Ben shot a worried glance at Raymond.

Raymond only angled his head toward the grease board. Ben followed his signal in time to see his dad draw a line that showed Thea, the center, pulling out of her position with an arrow directly at Number 17. His dad looked up at Thea with a spark in his eye.

Thea grinned like a wolverine bearing down on its prey.

Rich said, "Awesome. You guys got this? Every pass play, this will be our protection scheme. Let's see how Number 17 likes a mouthful of braids."

Everyone looked at Thea and her French braids. Thea blushed but held her chin high. Her eyes sparkled with pride. Ben smiled at her, and she smiled back.

Ben's dad rubbed out the Xs and Os with the sleeve of his jacket while everyone watched in silence. Ben's heart melted at the sight of his dad struggling with his weakened arms, but eventually he had cleared enough of the board to write a message that he held in his lap for all to see.

Winners NEVER Quit!!!
And Quitters NEVER Win!

A fire jumped to life inside of Ben. He looked around and saw the burning in his teammates' eyes as well. He remembered the sound of Rich's voice when he scolded Tuna. Rich *believed* they would win, and their dad had shown them how.

They jumped up at the sound of Raymond's whistle and did a brief warm-up. Ben's dad wheeled himself over to their sideline and planted himself on the fifty-yard line. In the excitement of their dad's appearance, Ben's brothers had forgotten about his possible concussion, and Ben wasn't about to remind them. His head ached, but he knew that was part of the game.

Rich called them all in and bellowed like a maniac. "You guys are *winners*! And you *never quit*! Thea, break 'em down."

Thea popped into the middle and shrieked like a banshee. "You heard Coach! We never quit! We're gonna tear them apart! We're gonna stomp them! We're gonna win this thing! Huh, huh, huh, huh, huh . . . Break it down!"

This time the team went wild.

The energy surged through them all like a current.

They had the ball. After the kickoff, Ben stormed the field with his offense. The board went up over Mr. Moreland's head, play nine, Green Bay, a rollout right pass with Torin the primary receiver on an out route. Rich wasn't wasting any time introducing Thea to Number 17.

Ben barked out the cadence, took the snap, and rolled right. Behind him, Ben heard the crack of pads like a rifle shot. Torin was open, and Ben threw it right away. Torin caught it and turned to crunch the defenders in his way. Ben looked back to see Thea badgering Number 17, hitting him, bouncing off, and attacking him again. After the whistle, Number 17 shoved her and turned to walk away.

Thea recovered and went right at him, shoved him in the back, and down he went. Flags flew in from two different officials. Fifteen yards for unsportsmanlike conduct.

On the sideline, Rich pulled his hair and screamed at the ref. "He hit her first! You must be blind!"

The penalty set them back, but they had the formula for success and marched down the field with some brilliant throws by Ben and some equally brilliant catches by Finn, Damon, Torin, Malik, and even Woody. They scored on a reverse with Damon and scored again on a long bomb to Finn. After each touchdown, Ben found his dad on the sideline to give him a hug.

His dad's smile and the light in his eyes said more than words.

The defense harassed Penn Yan to no end. They couldn't run, and when they attempted to pass, Thea was always there. She got a second interception halfway through the fourth quarter, giving Skaneateles the chance for a go-ahead drive.

Ben jogged onto the field looking up at the scoreboard, 26–20.

Rich called a hitch and go to Finn on the very first play. They had ended their last series with the same play for a touchdown. With the sudden change of the interception, Rich wanted to take advantage of the shock. He hoped to catch the Penn Yan secondary flat-footed.

Ben took the snap, pump-faked the hitch, and watched something incredible. Thea had pulled and charged straight for her rival, but instead of cracking pads, Number 17 leaped right over the top of her. Ben launched the ball, throwing for the spot he guessed Finn would be. Then he got a face full of Number 17.

The helmet to helmet hit knocked Ben flat. Another light show. In the NFL, Number 17 would have been ejected, but Ben's league followed the high school rules, which hadn't progressed that far, despite everyone's alleged concerns about head injuries. It had been a while since Number 17 had paid Ben a visit, and now he gloated over Ben.

The pass had been thrown off course, partly because of 17 and partly because of the wind in Ben's face. When the cry went through the Penn Yan defense, "Oskie! Oskie! Oskie!" Number 17 leered down at Ben. As he began to pick himself off the turf, 17 launched himself headfirst into Ben's head for a second time. This time Ben stayed down.

Rich sprinted onto the field screaming as he came. "Get seventeen off the field, ref! That's fifteen yards and the ball back for us! It was during the play!"

"Enough, Coach! He got blocked during the play! Another word from you and you'll get flagged!" The refs face turned purple.

Raymond appeared. "You okay, buddy? No, stay down. Don't get up. I want to give Thea a chance to catch her breath."

Rich knelt down beside them. "I swear I'm gonna knock that guy's block off."

"Rich, keep cool. You know how Dad wants us to treat the officials."

"Yeah. Yeah. Well, this guy's not an official. He's a chump. All game long, they've been hitting him after he's already gotten rid of it." Rich glared at the ref, then turned his attention to Ben. "Hey, Bo. We gotta stop meeting like this. How you feeling?"

"I'm okay. I'm lying here because Raymond wants to give Thea a chance to catch her breath."

Rich looked at Raymond. "Smart."

"You can call me that if my line stunts work on this next series."

"Did you run it by Dad?" Rich asked.

"He liked it."

"Good. Bo, headache?" Rich asked.

"No, I'm all good."

Rich peered down at him. "You don't look all good to me. Raymond?"

"Nah, he got his bell rung is all."

"That's what they told Dad."

Raymond gave his brother a dark look. "It's youth football, Richie, not the NFL."

"Tell that to seventeen."

"Do you want to win this game, or not? Cuz I know Dad didn't crawl out of that hospital bed to watch us back down."

Ben felt certain his brothers were about to fight.

Raymond looked around, and his face softened. "Come on, let's get him off the field."

They helped Ben up and escorted him to the sideline amid the polite applause of both sides of the stadium.

"They love you, Bo." Raymond chuckled.

"Because I just gave them the ball. They won't be cheering when I score."

"First we gotta stop them."

"Yup," said Ben. "First you gotta stop 'em."

Penn Yan put on a show.

On the sideline, Ben's dad gathered him, Woody, Torin, and Malik around his grease board. He drew what he'd already shown the left side of the line at halftime. Then he drew two new arrows showing Torin and Woody blocking the outside linebacker and the strong safety.

"So I don't go out?" Torin asked.

Ben's dad shook his head hard and tapped the arrow he'd just drawn. Then he pointed to Malik with his marker, making eye contact and grinning with anticipation before drawing a fat arrow from Malik's circle to Number 17. Ben's father scribbled down a word, underlined it five times before circling it.

The friends all craned their necks to see, but Ben's dad flipped the board around.

BOOM!!!

The friends all smiled at one another and patted Malik on the back.

Ben asked, "Should we tell Thea?"

His dad shook his head no and scribbled down another word.

Surprise!

Ben watched their defense slowly losing the battle and wondered if they'd even get the chance to blow up Number 17. If Penn Yan scored, it wouldn't matter anyway. Penn Yan drove the ball down to the eleven-yard line before the Defense 101 held true, putting their rivals in a fourth-and-eight predicament. Very few teams in the league even had a field goal team, but Penn Yan was one of them. As they trotted their kicking team out onto the field, Ben thought he might be sick after all.

"Of course he is!" Ben exclaimed when he saw Number 17 line up as the kicker.

Ben looked over to see if his dad saw what he saw. Raymond had bent down to consult with their dad. Their dad looked up at Raymond nodding vigorously and pointed toward the field.

Raymond ran out onto the field shouting, "Time-out! Time-out!"

The ref blew his whistle to stop the play and the clock.

Rich threw his hands up. "I'm gonna need those time-outs, Dad!"

Ben said what he knew his father was thinking. "We're not

gonna need them if they make this field goal, Rich."

To his credit, Rich nodded and said, "This is true."

Raymond came jogging back to the three of them. "I hope this works. I've got the feeling that seventeen won't miss if it doesn't."

"What did you do, Raymond?" Ben asked.

Raymond's face didn't inspire tremendous confidence. "I've got Luke Logan and Rohan running a stunt on the center."

Their dad nodded his approval, but the worry dragging down his expression brought Ben's spirits down as well.

The ref blew his whistle.

Number 17 looked down at the holder and gave him a nod. The holder returned the nod, turned, and flashed his hands at the center.

Ben felt the entire stadium holding its collective breath.

The center snapped the ball, and the holder pinned it to the tee.

Luke plowed the center over.

Rohan, that beautiful, tall, lanky, curly-headed kid, came looping around Luke like his pants were on fire. Number 17 took two big steps and swung his long muscular leg sending a thud to resonate in Ben's ears. But half an instant later, another thud rang out.

The ball leaped back at 17, took a high bounce, pitched back into the throng, and disappeared under a pile of bodies.

Ben nearly jumped out of his shoes. He kissed his dad and hugged his brothers as they danced around hooting. Their sideline exploded, and cheers rained down from the Visitors stands.

The celebration was short-lived, for Ben at least.

He looked up at the scoreboard.

Just 1:54 left on the clock.

Eighty-one yards to go.

Rich gathered his offense on the sideline.

While Ben's hands shook from nerves, Rich wore a stone-cold expression and spoke with calm certainty.

"This is what we've practiced for, guys, two-minute drill. Just go out there and do what you've done every day since August when we started this thing. We'll slow them down with some freeze plays, so be aware and be disciplined. Get out of bounds if you have the ball, and no penalties. If your man gets by you, do *not* hold. Let's go, guys. Win this thing."

The words and their tone comforted Ben. He glanced at his dad, who stared intently at him with a look of adoration that made him blush. His dad placed a hand on his heart, then pointed at Ben.

"I love you too, Dad." Ben squeezed his hand and ran out on the field.

He surveyed his offense, then looked at the board. Green Bay. Rich wanted to give 17 a taste of what he could expect for the final two minutes of the game. Ben felt giddy. If they could neutralize 17, he could pick their secondary apart.

He took the snap, rolled right, and hit Damon on a corner route. The free safety had an angle on Damon and hit him hard. Damon got out of bounds to stop the clock. It felt almost too easy. Ben looked back behind him to see Malik and Thea standing together watching as Number 17 picked himself up off the turf and skulked away.

Ben ran to them and slapped high fives.

Thea's face glowed. "I hit that sucker and BLAM! Out of nowhere comes Malik and puts him DOWN. I swear he knocked him silly."

"We'll see. C'mon, on the ball." Ben motioned with his head for them to follow and jogged up the field with his eyes on Mr. Moreland. Freeze play. Ben liked it.

He checked his teammates, making sure everyone was in the right place and giving them time to remind each other to stay still. He began his cadence keeping the same volume and rhythm.

"Blue seven, Blue seven . . . Down! Set . . . GO!"

No one jumped, but Ben wasn't done.

"Go! Go! *GO!*"

That got them! Half the Penn Yan defense jumped offsides. The ref marched five yards forward with the ball. Now the defense wouldn't anticipate the snap for a while. Between Damon's catch and the penalty, they only had fifty-eight yards to go and 1:47 on the clock. With two time-outs left, they could afford to run the ball.

Rich called play five, a direct snap to Malik, who lined up in the backfield next to Ben. This time, though, Rich crossed his arms in an X. Ben looked at Malik, who nodded back at him. Malik began the cadence, and Ben went into motion, toward the line and then to the left. Finn had lined up tight, right next to Tuna. Ben sailed past him and the cornerback guarding him. The Penn Yan coaches went wild on their sideline, jumping in the air and screaming.

"Cover him! COVER him!"

Thea snapped it to Malik. Malik tossed an easy pass to Ben. Ben snatched the ball out of the air and took off. The free safety listened to his coaches and had a head start on Ben. Number 17 had also been alerted, and from the corner of his eye, Ben could see him racing toward him at top speed.

He remembered Rich's speech and veered toward the sideline. At fifteen yards, he met the free safety at the sideline. Ben shot his left hand out, stiff arming the safety and driving his head down. When Ben's pinkie got caught in the safety's face mask, Ben instinctively slowed down, and because of that, the free safety forced him out of bounds. Ben twisted around and bent down to relieve the pressure on his finger.

That's when Number 17 hit him.

And Ben's bone snapped.

Ben gripped his hand and rolled back and forth on the turf doing his utmost to swallow back the screams boiling in his throat. Raymond appeared, and the sight of him somehow made it better. Then his dad appeared after having driven his wheelchair across the field, and Ben felt better yet. His dad looked at him intently and raised a fist, which said, "Be strong."

Meanwhile, Rich berated the ref. "He hit him *out of bounds*! You *had* to see that! You *had* to!"

"Looked clean to me, Coach. I go by what I see."

Ben's dad glared at Rich and shook his head to stop.

"By what you *see*? You've proven today that you don't *see anything*!" Rich appealed to the Penn Yan coach who stood nearby. "Am I right, Coach? Tell me if I'm wrong."

The Penn Yan coach turned without a word and melted into his team.

"See? You see *that*? He couldn't tell me because he knows I'm *right*!"

The ref said nothing. He simply pulled the yellow flag from his pocket and threw it straight up in the air. It landed with a small thud at Rich's feet. Their dad hung his head and shook it slowly back and forth.

Raymond cradled Ben's hand, but he looked up at their brother. "Nice move, Rich."

"Nice move by *him* you mean."

Ben wasn't crying, but hot tears of pain spilled down his cheeks. Raymond held Ben's hand up to distract Rich. The pinkie had been snapped in half, and the top half hung limp at a ninety-degree angle. Ben felt light-headed, but his brothers helped him up and steadied him on the long walk across the turf. Their dad drove his chair beside them. More polite applause rained down.

It made Ben sick.

Sol had his helmet on and threw the ball back and forth with Mr. Bennett.

"You got him, Raymond?" Rich asked.

"I got him, Rich. Go get us a touchdown." Raymond escorted Ben to the bench with his hand raised and the pinkie sagging.

Ben sat down on the bench. Raymond got two ice bags and packed the finger between them resting the whole mess on a pile of foam blocking shields. Ben's dad stayed close and took Ben's good hand in his own and gave it a squeeze.

"You good for a minute, Bo?"

Ben nodded that he was. Raymond nodded back and began

to rummage through the med kit.

Out on the field, Ben saw Sol throw a bubble screen to Malik. Malik hit a couple of defenders at the line and drove ahead for four more yards. Ben groaned. He knew Rich had to ease Sol into the game—you couldn't throw a kid in off the bench and expect him to throw a deep post—but they had the clock working against them too.

Ben couldn't see Rich, but he could hear him shouting for everyone to get on the ball. He looked up at the running clock as it dipped below a minute and a half. Sol threw a hitch pass on the next play, but Finn had to reach below his knees to catch it. He gained three yards but the cornerback tackled him in bounds, so Rich burned a time-out to stop the clock.

Ben's dad shook his head and wore a sad face, but he patted Ben's hand as if to say that everything would be all right. Rich jogged off the field with a grim expression.

"Got it." Raymond pulled a finger splint from the med kit with a roll of tape and held them out for their father to see.

Ben looked at his dad, who raised an eyebrow, shrugged, and pointed at Ben. It was his decision entirely.

"I can splint it and tape it, and you can go." Ben had never seen Raymond so serious before. "This isn't the NFL, Bo. No one's gonna think less of you if you don't. You've got a broken finger, and you're only a kid."

Ben hesitated, but only for a second. "Yeah, but I'm *his* kid. Do it, Raymond. Do it fast."

Raymond gave their dad one last look before straightening Ben's finger and clapping on the splint. Ben went dizzy from the pain but gritted his teeth and looked away as Raymond frantically wrapped the splint with tape.

Out on the field, Sol took the snap and rolled right. Somehow 17 got loose, and he quickly closed the gap on Sol, who searched for an open receiver with no idea of the danger. Ben saw Finn wide open on the deep post, and he willed Sol to see it too. Sol saw it and stopped to crank his hips around to throw the pass.

Just as Sol released the ball, Number 17 crashed into him with a bone-crunching blind-side hit. The ball wobbled up into the air and dropped like a gift from heaven into the waiting arms of Penn Yan's strong safety.

Ben's spirits sank.

Game over.

85

Except it wasn't over to Thea.

The safety who had intercepted the ball saw open ground and began to run. No one could blame him for taking the chance to seal the championship victory with a pick six. If he could have had the moment back, he would have fallen to the ground, protected the ball, and let his offense kneel with the ball for three snaps to win the game. But no one ever gets to have those moments back.

To Thea, who had football in her bones, the transition from an offensive player to a defensive one was as simple as hitting a light switch. She calculated the precise angle required for the intersection of their two paths in a nanosecond and took off like a heat-seeking missile. When she reached the safety running down the sideline, she didn't tackle him.

Instead, she punched the ball up in the air and dove on it as it hit the ground. They had a long way to go, and barely a minute to do it in, but they had a chance.

Ben ran out onto the field and didn't even feel his finger.

86

He slapped hands with Thea. "Awesome play, Thea!"

"I had to after seventeen got by us. He swam over me. Malik hit him, but he spun outside and disappeared like smoke in the wind. Don't worry, he won't get away with that again." Sweat streamed down her face.

"Do me a favor, okay?"

"Sure."

"Take some heat off those snaps." Ben held up his left hand. "It's broken. I know it's just a pinkie, but it hurts like heck."

"Don't worry. Soft as neck feathers."

He chucked her shoulder with his good hand, and they stepped into their positions.

On the sideline, Rich held his palms to the sky with wonder on his face, but he gave Ben two thumbs-up after Ben held up his taped finger. Rich turned to Mr. Moreland, who raised the board, play number one, a speed out to Woody. Ben had to admire Rich's thinking. They were attacking the kid who just got stripped of the ball, knowing he'd be distracted.

"Malik!" Ben shouted. "You gotta stay home! Thea, you're solo on this one!"

Thea looked back and gave him a nod.

Ben surveyed his offense, then the defense. Number 17 pointed at him to say he was coming for him. Ben began the cadence. Thea's snap had some air under it, soft as promised, but when it dropped into Ben's hands, a shock went up his arm. He pulled away instinctively and fumbled the ball. One of the ogres broke free and dove on it.

The ball squirted out like a watermelon seed. Jake dove on it and held tight. Ben looked to the sideline and saw Sol standing next to Rich, ready to go in. Ben understood. If he couldn't handle a snap, he couldn't play.

The clock was running.

"On the ball! On the ball!" he shouted. "Play one! Play one!"

His teammates scrambled for their positions, and he began the cadence the second the ref blew his whistle.

Thea snapped it just as soft. This time the shock didn't surprise him. He caught the ball and took off running. Even if Thea missed him completely, 17 couldn't catch him. Woody ran free with the safety trailing him two steps behind. Ben cranked it and hit Woody right in the hands.

The ball bounced up as if Woody had mistaken football for volleyball. Ben looked on in helpless terror as the cornerback dove for the ball. Fortunately, the strong safety had the same idea. The two of them collided, and the ball bounced off a helmet and to the ground.

Ben breathed a sigh of relief. Woody hung his head.

The clock stopped.

Only forty-seven seconds remained.

87

They faced a fourth down with fourteen yards to go.

Woody had made his cut at fifteen yards. It hurt to think about the first down they should have had, but Ben knew he had to move on.

The next board went up. Green Bay again, only this time Rich shouted, "Finn! Finn! Finn!"

Finn was normally third in the progression of the play, but Rich must have also seen Finn running free on Sol's interception play. Ben pointed at his brother and nodded. Beside Rich were Raymond and their dad. Their dad raised a tightly clenched fist in the air. Ben returned the signal and turned to his offense.

"Malik! Stay home! Torin, run the play! Solo again, Thea!" Ben would rather take his chances with 17 and have Torin out in the pattern.

He barked out the cadence, took the snap, and ran.

No one had covered Finn.

He was so wide open that Ben put some air under the ball to make it the easiest of catches. Finn turned, stopped, and made the catch almost as if it was a punt. Then he ran, but the secondary had rallied and Finn didn't get too far before being pulled down from behind.

Rich screamed for a time-out, their last. Rich jogged out onto the field and the offense huddled around him. Only thirty-six seconds remained on the scoreboard. Rich took a knee and smiled up at them.

"Fun, right? Okay, here's what we're gonna do. Woody, you look shaken, my man. I need you to switch positions with Malik because if he catches it, he can plow his way out of bounds." Rich hooked a finger on Malik's face mask and brought their heads together so that their eyes were four inches apart. "Okay, big guy. You gotta make the catch and get out of bounds. Make your break at *seven* yards. We're gonna line up and run the speed out till they stop it."

Rich let go of Malik's mask and looked around at them all. "First, we're gonna run a freeze play to get them back on their heels a bit. So you've gotta stay disciplined. *If* they don't jump, Ben, you just start the cadence over and we run the speed out on 'go.' If they get wise to the speed-out, they may call time-out and start to double cover Malik. If they do, we'll go back to the boards. I need every one of you to do your job. Run your patterns and make your blocks. Thea, you're gonna be all alone on that giant, but I know you can do it. Okay, bring it in."

Rich put a hand out in the middle of the huddle. Everyone did the same, creating a pile of hands. "This is your time, guys. This is everything you've worked for, and I know you're gonna bring it home. Champions on three. One, two, three . . ."

"CHAMPIONS!!!"

They went to the line. Ben surveyed his offense, then the Penn
Yan defense. Number 17 pointed at him again.

Ben said, "Bring it, if you can get by my girl."

Ben ignored him after that. He began his cadence, and
when he barked out "Go!" Number 17 lurched forward across
the line giving them five more yards without taking any time
off the clock.

They set up again. Ben called the cadence, took the snap,
rolled out to his right, and connected with Malik, who gained
nine yards before getting out of bounds. They quickly lined up
and ran it again, eight more yards. They were on the seven-yard
line with nineteen seconds on the clock.

Penn Yan called time-out.

Rich ran over to Ben and his teammates, who huddled
around him again.

"*Nice* work! Excellent work!" Rich's eyes burned bright.

"They're gonna double Malik now. That I promise you. So what we're gonna do is go back to Finn on the left side. On the snap, Finn, you run a slant. Tuna, you're blocking seventeen because this is quick and I need you to hit him low to get his hands down."

Rich took a deep breath. "If that doesn't work, I need you all to line up and look at the board. Okay? Hey, we are so close here. Let's finish them! Bring it in! Win, on three. One, two, three . . ."

"WIN!!!"

Ben gazed at the end zone, so close he could taste it.

He barked out the cadence, took the snap, and fired a pass at Finn. Tuna hit 17, but in the chest, almost propelling him higher in his leap that blocked the pass sending it up into the air. Ben didn't think. He reacted, caught the ball, and took off running. He looped around 17 and saw a wide-open path to the end zone. Finn's slant route had collapsed the defense.

Ben reached the five, the four, three, two, and one . . .

In that instant of elation, Ben got knocked sideways to the turf. His finger exploded with pain. Number 17 stood above him, gloating.

Ben wasted no time.

He leaped to his feet shouting to his teammates. *"On the line! On the line! On the line!"*

The clock read 00:09.

When the ref set the ball, the clock would run.

"Play one! Play one! Play one!"

His teammates scrambled like champions and got set on the line.

The ref set the ball, blew his whistle, and rolled his arm

setting the clock in motion. Ben took a breath and digested what he saw. His offense looked good, and the defense appeared ready to double Malik. Ben had an idea if they did.

He began his cadence. He had to stay calm. His teammates would hear confidence or panic. He knew this would be the last regular play of the game. All he had to do was take the snap before the clock hit zero.

". . . Go!"

The snap arrived. He ate the pain and sprinted to his right. Malik broke across the end zone, bracketed by two defenders, a risky throw. Damon was covered, Finn too. His line had sprung leaks, and several defenders closed in. He turned upfield, covered the ball, and lowered his pads. The impacts rattled his bones and sent a searing pain through his finger.

Buried under bodies, he had no way of knowing if he'd made it in. The officials peeled away the bodies and the ball, hugged tightly to Ben's chest, lay squarely on the goal line.

The official's hands went up.

Touchdown.

They quickly lined up and ran the same play again for the go-ahead conversion points. Ben found Damon open this time in the corner of the end zone when the man covering peeled off to play the run.

They dog-piled Damon in the end zone. The pile slowly melted into a boiling knot of kids. Up and down they bounced, like a bucket of BBs on a bumper. Ben and Thea found themselves facing each other bouncing in rhythm. Soon Tuna joined them. He had his jersey pulled up to his nose and his big belly bounced with them like a bowl full of jelly. Rohan joined in, then Woody, Malik, Finn, Jake and Luke, Omar, Harding, and

Damon. It wasn't long before the entire team bounced to the beat. Tuna began a chant that caught on and spread like gasoline on a campfire.

"Champs! Champs! Champs! Champs! Champs!"

Jake and Ro suddenly lifted Ben on their shoulders and the entire mob carried him to the sideline where his dad held up a fist, beaming in silence.

When the celebration subsided, after shaking hands with Penn Yan, and bathing in the joyful praise from the coaches, Ben found himself surrounded by his family, his mom and dad, brothers and sisters. They took many group pictures so as not to forget that day and what they called Ben's magnificent and courageous performance.

They all began a slow migration to the parking lot when Rich said, "Four brothers, quick meeting in the end zone."

"Rich," their mom groaned.

"Don't worry, Mom. Two minutes." Rich steered Ben around by the neck.

Their dad spun his wheelchair and followed with Raymond.

They reached the middle of the end zone before Rich stopped. "Huddle up here, guys."

"Rich, I'm gassed. . . ."

Rich bent over, put one arm around their dad's shoulder and the other around Ben's. "Just c'mere, and stop the belly achin'."

Raymond grumbled, but he closed the huddle.

Rich looked them each in the eyes before taking a deep breath and letting it out through puckered lips. "Guys, this is the last time the four brothers will be all on the same team.

We just won a championship, and, Bo, you're the man. Dad, none of us would be here without you, and, Raymond, defense wins games and you were killer. Me? I'm the magic. What can I say?"

They all laughed, and Ben felt the warmth running through him like a current. He returned the gaze of his dad, and he felt the love and the joy and the twist of sadness, because he knew Rich's words were true.

"This might not be the last." Raymond shook the huddle with his powerful shoulders. "Dad'll get better and we all might coach Ben in high school, right?"

Rich looked around at them all again. "No. This is it. So soak it in. Just soak it in. I love you guys, forever and infinity, right, Dad?"

Their dad nodded because that was his saying. They remained there for probably only a minute or two but what seemed a lifetime before they heard their mom's voice, loud and clear all the way from the parking lot.

The magic, and it was magic, was broken when they broke that huddle.

None of them spoke as they made their way to the vehicles. They loaded up and left Penn Yan's stadium behind them forever.

Ben's head ached and his finger throbbed, but that wasn't why he said what he said when they surged up the ramp and onto the highway. He said it because of the man in the front passenger seat, the man who could no longer drive, or walk, or eat, or talk. Ben loved the game as much as his brothers, and even his dad, but the price to be paid was just too high.

He would wrestle and play lacrosse, work hard in school, and maybe even follow his sister Rosie's footsteps to the Ivy league. He knew his dad and mom, sisters and brothers, would love him all the same, and that meant more than anything to him. So he said what he was thinking.

That this was his final season.

AUTHOR'S NOTE

Although *Final Season* is a work of fiction, much of the story is true. Because I have already used my own kids' names and personalities as the main characters in my Football Genius series, I've chosen to use everyone's middle name in this story, including my own middle name of John. Instead of the Green family, we are the Redds. Many of the other characters, especially Ben's teammates in football and lacrosse, are based on real kids with their real names and personalities. However, some, like Tuna and Woody, are entirely fictitious. I also added two characters, Thea and Rohan, who are my grandkids and too young to have been in the actual story, but whose personalities are spot on.

In some ways this book was easy to write. The story of all three of my sons' and our final season together as football coaches and player was what it was. If you'd like to see the actual *60 Minutes* piece, you can simply Google "Tim Green 60 Minutes." They really did show a touchdown run that Troy (Rich) told Draggan, the real *60 Minutes* producer, he would call. So, the story's structure and many of the fun and interesting elements were there for me to simply report.

In another way, though, writing this book was very difficult. Reliving the many painful moments and scenes of my slow but steady physical deterioration made the writing more like work than ever before. I will admit I didn't talk to my kids about how my having ALS made them feel. Instead, knowing them as well as I do, I interpreted their facial expressions, body language, and speech into what I believe is an accurate depiction of their thoughts.

At the heart of *Final Season* is the question of whether football is safe for kids to play. Our family was split on this, and I contend that there is no right answer, but only a choice that parents and kids must make according to their own beliefs and priorities. For me, it was the right decision, despite the cost. Football paid for my education and my kids' educations. Football opened doors in writing, business, television, and law. Football built our family's home on a beautiful lake in a picturesque town, and enough land for each of our kids to build their own homes. Also, being an NFL player made my biggest childhood dream come true.

My second big childhood dream was to become a writer. I have loved reading books since the third grade. To me, books were magic. They could take me away to another time and place. They could make me laugh and make me cry. In the heroes, I could see something of myself, or something I wanted to be. In the villains, I saw the things I didn't want to be. So I ached to make magic of my own one day. I was fortunate to have mentors and role models as an English major at Syracuse University who are giants in the world of literature, and others who are just plain brilliant.

So when ALS tried to take writing away from me, I fought back hard. One of my first symptoms of the disease was the loss of strength and coordination in my fingers. I had spent nearly thirty-five years writing and therefore typing every day. When I first started out, I longed for the day when the words would just flow from my mind through my fingers to the page. It took many years for that to happen, but it did, and I was loath to give it up.

Finally, my fingers became useless, but my thumbs still had some life left in them. I knew because I could text on my smartphone pretty well. I asked myself if I could write an entire three-hundred-page novel with my thumbs. My answer was, "Why not?" So in 2017 I wrote *The Big Game* on my phone with my thumbs. Then my thumbs went the way of my fingers. I had to find *something* that could get the stories out of my mind and onto the page. I went to a dear friend of mine, Nomi Bergman. I told her my dilemma, and she found a company called Bridging Voice. They had developed a system where I could stick a dot on my glasses so a sensor could pick up the movement of my head. With it, I could move the mouse across the screen, select a letter, and press a large button to type it.

I wrote my next book using that system, but my body continued to succumb to the disease, and I grew nervous about committing myself to another technology that would one day probably fail me. Around the same time I developed pneumonia and nearly died. To save me, the medical team had to give me an emergency tracheotomy, leaving me literally speechless. Advanced technology saved me again with a cutting-edge computer program that could take all the audio book recordings I'd narrated over the years and synthesize my voice. To do this I had to use another new technology, a Tobii Dynavox Eye Tracker.

The Tracker allows me to select letters by resting my gaze on the letters of a keyboard that takes up a little less than half of an iPad. Knowing that this method would avail itself to me for the rest of my life, I committed to the transition. Like all the previous methods for writing, it gets better with age, and the first chapter of *Final Season* took thrice the time as the last. Even with that improvement, I doubt I'll ever have the fluidity of typing with my fingers. Nevertheless, I will continue to write, for you and for me. I sincerely hope you enjoyed reading *Final Season* as much as I enjoyed writing it.